A DEAFE...

Finally, Carter's self-control meter blew a gasket. "THERE'S A GOAT IN THERE, JORGE!" he cried. "¡UN CHIVO! ¡UN CHIIIIIIVO!"

Then, shrugging me off like a leaf, he charged the bushes in what can only be described as a bloodthirsty frenzy! Fangs out, deadly razor-sharp claws gleaming dangerously in the moonlight!

"He . . . *gone!*" gasped Carter, big eyes bugging with bewilderment. "Jess left his hat! An old goatskin hat! Dat's why I smelled old goat!"

"And *I* smell an ignoramus!" barked an annoyed disembodied voice.

For a dizzy second, I had no idea where it could have possibly come from. But then my eyes nearly bugged out of my face as I realized there was only *one* possibility!

It was the hat.

The sombrero.

The thing had *talked*!

ALSO BY GEORGE LOPEZ AND RYAN CALEJO:

ChupaCarter
ChupaCarter and the Haunted Piñata
ChupaCarter and the Curse of La Llorona

CHUPACARTER
AND THE SCREAMING SOMBRERO

GEORGE LOPEZ
WITH
RYAN CALEJO

ILLUSTRATED BY
SANTY GUTIÉRREZ

VIKING

VIKING

An imprint of Penguin Random House LLC
1745 Broadway, New York, New York 10019

First published in the United States of America by Viking,
an imprint of Penguin Random House LLC, 2024
First paperback edition published 2025

Copyright © 2024 by George Lopez
ChupaCarter and the Curse of La Llorona excerpt copyright © 2025 by George Lopez

Penguin Random House values and supports copyright. Copyright fuels creativity, encourages diverse voices, promotes free speech, and creates a vibrant culture. Thank you for buying an authorized edition of this book and for complying with copyright laws by not reproducing, scanning, or distributing any part of it in any form without permission. You are supporting writers and allowing Penguin Random House to continue to publish books for every reader. Please note that no part of this book may be used or reproduced in any manner for the purpose of training artificial intelligence technologies or systems.

Viking & colophon are registered trademarks of Penguin Random House LLC.
The Penguin colophon is a registered trademark of Penguin Books Limited.

Visit us online at PenguinRandomHouse.com.

The Library of Congress has cataloged the hardcover edition as follows:
Names: Lopez, George, 1961– author. | Calejo, Ryan, author. | Gutiérrez, Santy, 1971– illustrator.
Title: ChupaCarter and the screaming sombrero / George Lopez with Ryan Calejo ;
illustrated by Santy Gutiérrez.
Description: New York : Viking, 2024. | Series: ChupaCarter ; book 3 |
Audience: Ages 8–12. | Audience: Grades 4–6. | Summary: When Ernie's dad is accused of stealing artifacts related to the legendary El Dorado gold, Jorge and his friends set out to clear his name and run into a fiendish ring of thieves along the way.
Identifiers: LCCN 2023058420 (print) | LCCN 2023058421 (ebook) |
ISBN 9780593466032 (hardcover) | ISBN 9780593466049 (trade paperback) | ISBN 9780593466056 (ebook)
Subjects: CYAC: Stealing—Fiction. | El Dorado—Fiction. | Chupacabras—Fiction. |
Hispanic Americans—Fiction. | Mystery and detective stories. | Humorous stories. |
LCGFT: Detective and mystery fiction. | Humorous fiction. | Novels.
Classification: LCC PZ7.1.L6678 Co 2024 (print) | LCC PZ7.1.L6678 (ebook) | DDC [Fic]—dc23
LC record available at https://lccn.loc.gov/2023058420
LC ebook record available at https://lccn.loc.gov/2023058421

ISBN 9780593466049

1st Printing

Printed in the United States of America

LSCC

Edited by Jenny Bak | Design by Opal Roengchai | Text set in Athelas

This book is a work of fiction. Any references to historical events, real people, or real places are used fictitiously. Other names, characters, places, and events are products of the author's imagination, and any resemblance to actual events or places or persons, living or dead, is entirely coincidental.

The publisher does not have any control over and does not assume any responsibility for author or third-party websites or their content.

The authorized representative in the EU for product safety and compliance is Penguin Random House Ireland, Morrison Chambers, 32 Nassau Street, Dublin D02 YH68, Ireland, https://eu-contact.penguin.ie.

To the moon, thank you for lighting my way!
—G. L.

To Yiya
—R. C.

To my father, for teaching me the values that
I now try to pass on to my son
—S. G.

There are some things you just don't see every day.

This *definitely* qualified as one of those things.

Spoiler alert: we found what we'd been looking for.

And it was beyond *anything* any of us could have ever imagined . . . But I want to say up front that this isn't just another story about finding lost treasure.

This is a story about finding the only *true* treasure in this world. The only treasure out there really worth risking your neck to find.

This is a story about *friendship*.

Carter's seeKret

HiLLS

WUDZ

Tasty Trezure

SW

CHAPTER 1

"Hold up!" I lowered the junky old metal detector and turned to Ernie in surprise. "Are you talking about *the* El Dorado?"

Ernie looked at me like I'd sat on his last Twinkie. "Uh, *hello*? Earth to Jorge! What do you think I've been talking about this whole time?"

"Honestly? I have no idea," I confessed. "I sort of tune you out when you start babbling about Star Trek or ancient history."

The three of us—that's me, Ernie, and Liza—were prowling around the outskirts of Ernie's parents' sprawling fifteen-acre ranch, on the hunt for hidden treasure.

But so far, we'd done an awful lot of hunting and very little *finding*.

What you'd expect to find on a treasure hunt...

What we actually found...

A few yards away, Liza, who was passing a cracked, not-so-magical metal-detecting wand over a clump of deer grass, grinned at me like, *You're too much, Jorge.*

"I'm not kidding," I said, wiping sweat off my face. "History makes me sleepy. I mean, you've seen what happens in Mrs. Green's class when she starts talking about the Industrial Revolution. It knocks me right out!"

"Well, he's not lying," she told Ernie. "I've had to poke him awake *five* classes in a row now."

"That was YOU?!" I shouted. "Liza, how could you do that? I'm a growing boy! You could throw my entire sleep cycle out of whack!"

Sighing, Liza showed me the bottoms of her eyeballs, then turned her attention back to the patch of scraggly grass. "If you want to count sheep in class," she said with a hint of annoyance, "then I suggest you join the *kindergartners* after lunch..."

"I already tried that!" I admitted. "But Mrs. Herrera told me I was too big for the blankets they hand out!"

"I sincerely hope you're joking, Jorge."

I wasn't. But she didn't need to know that.

Behind us, the fiery face of a blazing New Mexican sun was glaring down from above the pointy peaks of pine trees. Squinting against the glare, I turned back to Ernie, who was busy hunting for a mythical city of gold underneath a tiny clump of red-and-white mushroom caps.

"Anyway, let me get this straight," I said. "You were actually expecting to find El Dorado *five minutes* from your house?"

Not that it would've surprised me much with my boy Ernie. Over the last couple of weeks, the kid had become totally obsessed with that silly legend. I mean, it was getting almost as bad as his Star Trek obsession, and that was saying something.

Ernie sighed. "If you'd paid attention to anything I've been saying, Jorge, then you would know that all the most reliable source material places El Dorado somewhere in southwest New Mexico. So why not in my backyard?"

"Why not mine?" I countered.

He shrugged like he couldn't think of a good reason. "Why not? You want to check yours next?"

"No, Ernie! I don't! Because we're not going to find El Dorado in *anybody's* backyard! And especially not with these flea market metal detectors that you bought on eBay for a buck each!" I shook mine and a shiny plastic piece came loose and clunked to the ground. "See what I mean?"

"You know, I always just assumed El Dorado was somewhere in South America," said Liza, brushing sweat from her eyes.

Indiana Ernie shook his head. "Nah, that's just one of the many false stories. I've also heard Mexico and Guatemala, and I even saw a documentary last week that claimed it was on some tiny island in the Caribbean—St. George's Caye, I think." Ernie shrugged. "That's the thing with these überfamous legends—different versions pop up all over the place, and the locals usually end up putting their own spin on them. So yeah, there are El Dorado stories all over Central and South America, and they're all a bit different."

"But if it's like that, then how do you know which is the authentic one?" I asked.

"Usually, the oldest story is the most authentic."

"Which, in the case of El Dorado," said Liza, "would be the story of the Spanish explorer Francisco Vázquez de Coronado, who led an unsuccessful expedition through New Mexico, searching for the seven cities of gold."

Surprised, I turned to Liza. "Hey, how did you know that?" Honestly? I would never have guessed there was any room left for fairy tales in that scientific-fact-filled brain of hers.

"Because I was listening *three minutes ago* when Ernie was talking about it, Jorge!"

"Oh."

"Actually, Francisco's story isn't the oldest," said Ernie. "That's what I was trying to get to before *someone* rudely interrupted me."

He shot me a real meaningful look, but I shrugged it off.

Then—as was quickly becoming an every-minute-of-every-day type of thing with E-dog—he started talking about El Dorado again. Only this time, I actually paid attention.

Here's the short version:

Jorge's El Dorado Power Points

1) About five months ago, a team of archaeologists unearthed an ancient Aztecan burial site somewhere in central Mexico near the Popocatépetl volcano.

2) In one of the tombs, they discovered a sarcophagus that belonged to an Aztecan priest and contained dozens of jade

tablets that explained the meanings of previously unknown Aztecan symbols.

3) This made it possible for language experts all over the world to decipher a whole mess of previously untranslated Aztecan codices.

4) A bunch of these translated writings (some of which predated Francisco's expedition by hundreds of years) mentioned the legendary El Dorado.

5) Apparently, El Dorado had less to do with a city of gold and more to do with a vengeful Aztecan bruja (witch) who plundered seven of the most prominent Aztec cities at the height of their power and hid their wealth from them as a punishment for the greed of their leaders.

"According to a few of the most recently translated codices," Ernie continued, "the only person who ever discovered the secret location of the treasure was this kid—a sort of beggar-thief—who tried to steal some from la bruja. Supposedly, though, she laid this *horrible* curse on him, and he was never seen again!"

"That wasn't very nice of her," I said.

Ernie shrugged, absentmindedly swinging his metal detector around, searching for El Dorado underneath an anthill now. "Anyway, according to some other manuscripts, the witch left behind three clues to the whereabouts of the treasure, in the form of three cursed items."

"Wait. How cursed are we talkin'?" I asked, suddenly sort of interested.

Ernie's voice dropped to a creepy whisper. "*Extremely* cursed!"

"What were the items?" Liza wanted to know.

"A bejeweled Aztecan dagger carved from a single slab of meteoric rock, a large black sombrero of unknown origin, and a riddle written on an ancient piece of amatl paper by la bruja's own hand."

"What's the riddle?" I asked, and instantly saw a goofy grin split Ernie's lips, like he'd been desperately hoping one of us would ask.

He quoted it now, word for word, like it was one of Captain Kirk's famous lines: "'Cross the waters without a greedy hand. Walk the path without a greedy eye. Stab the heart of greed. Offer a worthy sacrifice and seize the true treasure that lies before you!'"

"Sounds sort of ominous," I had to admit.

"Sounds *super* ominous!" he hissed excitedly. Apparently, he was pretty stoked about the riddle's ominousness. "But get this! From all the writings I've come across, the riddle has something to do with the witch's challenges! See, the bruja was said to have protected the treasure with a series of deadly challenges, so that anyone seeking the treasure would have to prove themselves worthy of it. From what my dad and I have been able to dig up, the ancient Aztecs believed that only with all three clues could someone break the curse and discover the secret location of the vast treasure—a place the witch had named El Dorado." Ernie's eyes were bugging so far out of his face in excitement that I was half-afraid one might roll right out. I had my hand ready to catch it in case one did. "But here's the best part: all three artifacts are currently less than a fifteen-minute bike ride away, because the museum is in town and already setting up shop!"

The museum he was talking about was the Museum of Natural Wonders, this big fancy institution in Chicago.

See, if you thought Ernie was obsessed with El Dorado, just wait until you hear about his dad...

That man had taken El Dorado Syndrome (yes, I'd given the condition an official name) to a whole 'nother level. Recently he'd convinced (i.e., *bribed* with a series of huge donations) the museum's board of directors to do a pop-up show with some of their world-famous exhibits down here in New Mexico.

Obviously, their *El Dorado* exhibit was the main attraction, and from everything I'd heard in the buildup to the show, Ernie's dad was basically drooling all over himself to get an up close and *extremely* personal look at the three famous artifacts.

And now I knew why.

Anyway, the head curator of the museum was personally setting the whole thing up at the local civic center, which Ernie's dad had rented out for the weeklong event.

"My dad actually talked to the curator last night to see if he would let us examine the artifacts ourselves," Ernie rambled on. "Y'know, with some cutting-edge techniques we've been researching. But he said the guy acted like a total dope—basically went ballistic on him just for asking, and threw him out. My dad told me not to worry, though. He promised we'd get our hands on the artifacts one way or another."

"Hold up. Let me see if I follow," I said. "So

El Dorado is where this—I'm assuming *super-powerful*—bruja hid the treasure of the seven Aztec cities?"

"Correct."

"And El Dorado hasn't been found or even *glimpsed* for the last thousand years or so?"

"Correct again."

"And according to the oldest and most reliable Aztec writings, no one can find El Dorado without the three cursed artifacts, right?"

"You're three for three, Jorge!"

"And we obviously don't have those artifacts on us at the moment, correct? Does that make me four for four?"

"Uh, *of course* we don't have the artifacts, Jorge... I just told you the museum has them."

"That's what I thought I heard you say. So quick question: WHY IN THE CHEESE-AND-BEAN-FILLED ENCHILADA DID YOU DRAG US OUT HERE IN SEARCH OF A TREASURE THAT HASN'T BEEN DISCOVERED IN OVER A MILLENNIUM AND CAN *ONLY* BE FOUND BY SOMEONE WHO HAS ALL THREE CURSED ARTIFACTS, WHEN WE CLEARLY DON'T EVEN

HAVE *ONE*, AND IT'S HOTTER THAN A PIZZA OVEN IN HADES OUT HERE?!" Yeah, I was in kind of a bad mood. But that's only because I'd leaked enough sweat to fill half the Pacific Ocean, and my face felt like it was getting the same deep-fry treatment as chicharrones right before they're tossed into a snack bag. "I mean, this is the textbook definition of a wild goose chase! Actually, it's even worse than that! This is closer to a wild goat chase!"

I had plenty more to say, too. But before I could, the patch of bare ground in front of us suddenly erupted like a mini-volcano, and out leapt the shaggy, scraggly form of a ginormous bloodthirsty monster!

CHAPTER 2

Okay, so I lied. It wasn't some ginormous bloodthirsty monster. Well, in all fairness, he *is* sort of bloodthirsty (in a very literal sense), but he's definitely no monster.

It was just Carter. My best bud.

"Somebody say 'goat'?" he asked excitedly, blinking his mismatched blue and green eyes around at us.

Okay, don't scream. Yes, Carter's a real-life chupacabra. But he also happens to be the nicest, kindest, sweetest soul this side of pretty much anywhere.

We'd met on the roof of my grandparents' house one night while I was dodging my grandma's empanadas and missing L.A. and Carter was running for his life from a pack of bloodsucking vampire dogs.

You know the old expression "Don't judge a book by its cover"? It applies double in Carter's case. Sure, on the outside, the dude might look fit for a horror movie, but on the inside, he's all squishy teddy bears and rainbow-colored marshmallows.

Don't let those foot-long razor-sharp fangs scare you. Well, unless of course you happen to be a goat. Then you should totally let his fangs scare you. (And you should probably start running, too.)

"Carter! You scared the nachos out of us!" I shouted.

A long purple tongue slid out from between Carter's fangy teeth as he licked his lips. "And where'd dey go? I didn't eat no lunch yet, Jorge!"

Liza, who was still trying to catch her breath, said, "Carter, weren't you just all the way on the *other* side of the field? How'd you even get here?!"

He gave her a look like, *Silly human. I'm a chupacabra. Which means I'm basically Superman with a pettable, full-body coat.*

"Chupacabras burrow, 'member? But ¡mira!" He stuck a huge, clawed hand out between the three of us. "I found da treasure!"

Yeah, the big guy had been treasure hunting with us. Though

he clearly had a *very* different definition of the word "treasure."

"Carter, that's *not* treasure." Ernie sighed. "Those are just some crusty old bottle caps."

The chupacabra's thick eyebrows pressed together in something like a furry question mark. "But dey metal."

"Yeah, so?"

"Jorge tole me gold and silver was treasure, and dey both metal."

"Yeah, so?"

"So why dis metal not treasure?"

"He does bring up an interesting point," I had to admit.

"And on that note," said Liza, clicking off her metal detector, "I think we should call it quits on our Indiana Jones work for the day. I still have some homework to finish."

Off to the west, the sun had sunk slowly behind the tops of the tall trees, and their telescopic shadows stretched out long ahead of us as we started back to Ernie's.

"Who's up for some El Dorado–inspired poppers?" asked my El Dorado–obsessed amigo.

CHUPACARTER AND THE SCREAMING SOMBRERO

"ME!" Carter and I shouted in unison. Yeah, we both had a thing for oven-fresh snacks.

"What's in them?" Liza wanted to know.

"Jalapeños, nondairy cream cheese and cheddar cheese, bread crumbs, and a slice of golden beet. They're totally vegan-friendly."

"In that case, count me in!" she said with a hungry grin, which brought our hungry grin count up to a grand total of four. But, unfortunately, that was the last time any of us would grin that day. Because as we pushed our way through the hedge of bushes that ringed the green sweep of manicured lawns surrounding Ernie's parents' house, we saw something *terrible* . . .

It was Ernie's dad.

He was being arrested!

CHAPTER 3

Watching Ernie's dad get handcuffed and shoved into the back of a police car had me totally shook. And it wasn't because I hadn't seen someone get arrested before. I had. In fact, it happened pretty often back in my old neighborhood.

But the soft-spoken, generous, and (if I'm being completely honest) borderline *dorky* dad of one of my best friends? Yeah, that was a total shocker.

And why had the police arrested him? Get this: for stealing from that fancy-schmancy Chicago museum—the museum he himself had shelled out mad dough to bring to town!

And even more mind-blowing? He was being accused of stealing the very same artifacts that Ernie had just been telling us about! The dagger, the bruja's riddle, and the sombrero!

You couldn't make this stuff up. But almost as shocking was how quickly the local TV news stations had run with the story, and how quickly the townspeople had turned on him.

Exhibit A: my sweet old nana.

"He's as guilty as the first fox out of a henhouse!" Paz shouted later that night as the three of us sat down for dinner.

"You don't think we should at least give him the benefit of the doubt?" I protested.

She considered that for a sec, her forehead creasing, then shooed the thought away with her fork. "Nah..."

"How's Ernie doing?" my grandpa asked, cutting himself a big yellow wedge of tamale.

I sighed. "Not good. Before I left his house, he offered me half of his last strawberry shortcake ice cream bar."

A look of confusion crinkled the sun-toasted corners of my abuelo's eyes. "But that was nice of him. That's a good thing, no?"

"Not for Ernie!" I said. "He never shares his ice cream bars with anybody! And *especially* not strawberry shortcake! It means he's all messed up inside!"

"Probably, 'cause he just realized his dad's a crook," Paz chimed in.

"Grandma!" I snapped, but she just rolled her shoulders at me like, *The truth hurts, kid.*

"Bueno, let's not jump to any conclusions," said Patricio. "There's this little-known tradition in the US legal system known as 'innocent until proven guilty.' Maybe we give that a try?"

"Ha! That's a sucker's game!" said my grandma. "I always start with guilty. It saves time." She leaned comfortably back in her chair. "Besides, Ernie's dad might as well have a giant sign over his head with the word ¡CULPABLE! flashing in bright neon lights. That weaselly looking curator saw the whole thing. They even got video footage of him going *in* and coming *out* of the museum at the exact time of the robbery! What more do you two want—a handwritten confession?"

My grandma sipped on her cup of agua fresca.

"Look, I'm not judging the man," she said. "If I actually believed I could find the treasure of El Dorado with those crusty old artifacts, I'd go into the museum and steal them myself. But we have to face reality: technology has made high-stakes museum burglaries a losing bet these days. That's why I never got into the business myself."

My grandma as a high-stakes cat burglar. I could almost see it now...

"Anyway, I don't even need any evidence," said Paz. "I *know* he's guilty."

Annoyed, I pushed my plate away. "Grandma, what are you talking about? How could you possibly know that?"

"Because all rich people are crooks! *That's* how!"

"Por Dios, Paz," my grandpa groaned, setting his knife and fork down on the table.

"Uh, stereotype much?" I said to her.

"Stereotype? ¡No inventes! The only *typing* I've ever done was one time on your grandfather's old computer when I made my own online blog called *All White People Dance the Same*."

Sighing, I threw my hands up. I mean, what could you even say to that?

CHAPTER 4

Half an hour later, Carter and I were hanging out on the rough, sandpapery shingles of my grandparents' roof, gazing up at the bright full moon while gusts of dry, desert-y air occasionally rustled my hair and Carter's shaggy coat. I love moon watching. If there's one thing in the world that calms me down, one thing that makes me feel safe and watched over and optimistic about what tomorrow might have in store, it's moon watching.

For as long as I can remember, no matter how upside down my life got, no matter how chaotic or messy, the moon was always there for me, always in the same spot, at the same time—and it would always find me. But tonight, something was off. I just didn't feel that same deep sense of tranquility I usually felt when I stared up at that familiar smiling yellow face.

It wasn't hard to figure out why. I felt *terrible* for Ernie...

"Everything my grandma said was true!" I blurted to Carter. "I saw it on the news myself. They do have video footage of Ernie's dad going in and out of the museum, and the curator himself said that Ernie's dad attacked him and ransacked the exhibit!"

It would probably end up being the most open-and-shut case ever. I mean, the evidence was practically poking you right in the eyes!

It was wild to think about, but in all of eight hours, Mr. Nez had gone from being one of the most highly respected people in the community to one of the least. It wasn't only my grandma who was trashing him; half the town was, too! People were pretty much split fifty-fifty, kind of like Team DC vs. Team Marvel.

And let's face facts: Ernie had lived a way more sheltered life than I had. He hadn't grown up in L.A. with no dad, no food on the table some days, no presents under the tree some Christmases. He'd never been kicked out of his apartment in the middle of the night because his mom couldn't make rent that month. He hadn't watched his mother cry for nearly two weeks straight because she couldn't seem to find a job. The world had made me tough. On the outside, at least. But Ernie? Not so much... And if this whole thing was hard for me to handle, I could only imagine what it was doing to poor Ernie.

"I guess I can understand why Mr. Nez did it," I said with a depressed shrug. "He and Ernie were so obsessed with that stupid treasure. According to Ernie, his dad's been fascinated with it since he was *our* age. That's what got him interested in the mining business." My gaze slid over to Carter, who had been unusually quiet tonight. In the gloom, the chupacabra's eyes glowed like two miniature moons.

"What would you do if you found a treasure like that?" I asked him.

The shoulders of the big guy rose and fell like he'd never thought about it. "I dunno. What would you do?"

"Me? Eh, I might buy a thing or two..." I said.

Carter's thin, kangaroo-shaped face was pinched with thought, and after a moment he said, "I think I probably give the treasure back."

Which made me shake my head. "Give the treasure back? Give it back to *who*?"

"Whoever it belonged to before I found it," Carter replied, as if it was the most obvious thing in the world.

It was probably the strangest answer anyone had ever given to that question. I guess chupacabras didn't play by that most sacred of playground rules: *finders keepers.*

We fell into silence again, and the wind blew and the world was dark and quiet. Finally, I said, "Did you know that El Dorado is supposedly right here in New Mexico? Ernie told me once that according to legend, there was enough treasure in El Dorado to fill the Grand Canyon."

The chupacabra didn't answer.

"The Grand Canyon... Can you imagine that?" I almost couldn't. That would amount to, like, an *ocean* of treasure. "Yeah, I guess I can see why Ernie's dad did it..."

"He didn't do it, Jorge," Carter said after a moment.

I blinked at him. "What do you mean?"

"Ernie's dad is innocent."

"Dude, I told you already. There were cameras. There's footage. They have an *eyewitness*!"

He shrugged like it didn't matter. "I know he's innocent. Don't care what anybody's eyeballs say."

"What makes you so sure?"

"Because Ernie told us so."

"You mean, you're just taking Ernie's word for it?"

The big guy nodded.

"But, Carter, it's *his dad*... What's he supposed to say?"

"Friends don't lie to friends, Jorge. So Ernie no lie to us. And he knows his dad best. Dat's how *I* know his dad didn't do it."

For several seconds I just stared at him, shaking my head. I honestly didn't know what to say to that. I mean, talk about being naive... It was almost adorable, if you think about it.

Wouldn't it be awesome to live in a world like that, though? A world where nobody lied and you could believe everything somebody told you just because you were buddies?

I wish I could trust people like Carter does, I thought. But then I remembered who my grandma was—and how sneaky and conniving she could be—and I realized it was way better for me that I didn't.

Still, it got me thinking. At the end of the day, it *was* just a choice, wasn't it? I could just take Ernie's word for it, too, if I really wanted to. After all, he was one of my best friends.

And who knows? Maybe his dad hadn't done it. Maybe Mr. Nez's doppelgänger had strolled into the civic center that night and stolen the El Dorado artifacts, and Mr. Nez had gotten all the blame. Was it likely? Heck no! But if Carter could believe Ernie, why couldn't I?

And why *shouldn't* I? Wouldn't I expect him to believe *me* if it was my grandma who had been accused and I was the one saying she was innocent?

On second thought, that was a terrible example. If anyone accused Paz of *anything*, I'd be the first one to believe them. And I'd be proven right, too.

"You know . . . now that I think about it," I said, talking aloud, "there isn't any video footage of Mr. Nez actually *stealing* anything. They hadn't installed security cameras inside yet. There's just footage of him walking into the museum with his briefcase and then walking back out a little while later. I mean, if you really want to get technical about it, this whole thing boils down to the curator's word against Mr. Nez's. And the guy could totally be lying, couldn't he?"

Now I had the chupacabra's attention. That gigantic fur-covered head was nodding up and down enthusiastically, and those gigantic razor-sharp fangs were poking out in a goofy grin.

"I think da curator *is* lying, Jorge!" Carter whispered excitedly, the moonlight casting a silvery haze around the pointy tips of his bat-like ears. "Ernie's dad is innocent!"

At least until proven guilty, right?

And suddenly, I had a genius idea!

CHAPTER 5

"It's so simple! We just have to prove your dad's innocence!" I shouted the next day at Ernie's as I laid out my plan for the gang. We were all hanging out in E-dog's Star Trek–themed bedroom—Carter chilling on the Star Trek beanbag chair, Liza sitting on the Star Trek throw rug, and Ernie sprawled miserably out on his USS *Enterprise* bed with the Star Trek sheets and Captain Kirk comforter. So far, I had gotten some half-interested smiles, but no real enthusiasm for my total *Eureka!* moment.

Ernie let out a tired sigh. "What are you talking about, Jorge?"

"Oh, c'mon, don't look at me like I'm fanged and crawled out of the woods somewhere!" My gaze slid to the confused face of the chupacabra. "No offense. Seriously, though. We all believe he's innocent, don't we?"

"Of course my dad's innocent!" Ernie snapped.

"Uh, yeah, of course . . ." agreed Liza. (Though, for the record, she didn't sound quite as convinced as Ernie.)

"Exactly!" I said. "So all we need to do is scrounge up a bit of evidence proving what we all already know is the truth, and the police will have to let him go!" Hey, at least that was how it worked in all my grandparents' telenovelas.

"And how, pray tell, do you suggest we go about finding that evidence?" asked Liza, raising her trademark skeptical eyebrow.

"C'mon, peeps! I can't come up with *all* the great ideas!" I complained. "Let's put our thinking caps on!"

Another confused frown was tugging at the furry ends of Carter's lips. "But I don't got no cap."

"Dude, it's a metaphor," I tried to explain.

But vampire Chewbacca's frown only got frownier. "I don't got one of those, either . . ."

"All right," I said to the gang. "First things first. Before we go running off trying to prove Mr. Nez's innocence, let's see exactly what they've got against him."

So that's exactly what we did. We hopped on Ernie's laptop and ran a quick online search. One of the local news websites listed the charges as assault, resisting arrest, and grand larceny.

"And look what this article says." Liza clicked open another link. "According to several reports, a whole bunch of neighbors claim to have heard a series of odd, ear-piercing shrieks at the exact time of the robbery."

"Probably the curator screaming for help," I guessed.

"That's what I figured, too. Only look over here." She pointed with Ernie's USS *Enterprise*–themed cursor. "The curator claims he heard the same screams but has no idea who it was."

That was pretty weird. And pretty interesting...

Liza clicked another link, and this was the headline that popped up on the monitor:

MUSEUM STAFF ASSAULTED!

HEAD CURATOR, IRA BADDENSWORTH, BOPPED ON THE HEAD BY A MALLET, CLAIMS THE MAN HIMSELF.

"See?! That's how I know my dad is innocent!" shouted Ernie. "He'd never bop anyone on the head with anything!"

"Then this curator dude is making the whole thing up?"

"Do Vulcans have inner eyelids?"

Lost, I looked at Liza. "Do they?"

She gave me a sheepish nod, like she was embarrassed she knew that. "They do, Jorge . . . they do."

Ernie looked pleadingly around at us. "My dad didn't do it. The curator's *lying*!"

Man, there was just something so honest in those big brown eyes of his . . . Ernie really believed this. I mean, like, *really* believed it. His dad was completely innocent in his mind.

Okay, fine. I'd made up my mind to trust my buddy and that was exactly what I was going to do.

"Then we start with the curator!" I said.

CHAPTER 6

The civic center was as busy as a beehive when we arrived. It reminded me of a big town fair, except nobody looked like they were having any fun. And in the middle of all the frantic, flustered busyness, we found the man we were looking for: the museum's head curator, Mr. Ira Baddensworth.

The curator was a pale, weaselly-faced man with pinched beady eyes and a pinched little mouth. Even his arms and shoulders appeared to be pinched back along his bony spine, and he stood very straight up, as if someone had jammed a yardstick up the back of his stiff button-down shirt.

Currently, he was barking orders at a team of sweaty workers as they hauled what looked like King Tut's tomb out of a gigantic wooden shipping crate.

"Pay attention to what you're doing, BLOCKHEAD!" he roared. "And for the queen's sake, be gentle with it! That artifact is worth more than all your lives—*COMBINED!*"

"Well, this is going to be fun," I whispered as we came up behind Mr. Curator Dude. Liza introduced us and asked Ira if he had a few minutes to talk. But you could tell from the way he whirled around, staring down at us like we were a couple of cockroaches that had found our way onto his chicken enchilada, what his answer was going to be.

"Obviously *not!*" he snapped. "I don't even have a *second!* Opening night is nearly upon us and this place might as well be declared a disaster zone!" His icy green eyes narrowed fiercely on me. "Oh, but our doors *will* open on opening night! We will not be intimidated. No, not even in the face of brazen criminality!"

Turning back around, he barked out a fresh batch of orders to his staff and even hit a guy in the back with a fat marker he'd picked up from the floor.

But a few moments later, when he glanced back at us again and saw that we hadn't moved and realized that we were going absolutely *nowhere* until we got to talk to him, he let out a loud, irritated sigh and said, "Oh, follow me! Follow me!"

He started across the main hall at practically a jog, rudely shoving people out of his way and barking out more orders as he led us into what I guessed was his office—a cramped little room littered with shipping boxes.

"Please make this brief," he grumbled in a thin, sort of nasally voice that actually said *Please just go away*. "What is so colossally important that you felt compelled to interrupt my most vital work?"

Híjole, what an ego on this guy. You'd think he was on the brink of solving nuclear fusion or something.

"Well, we had a few questions about the night

of the robbery," said Liza, and instantly his already-annoyed face screwed up like she'd smacked him.

"Of course you did!" he roared. "That's the only thing anyone in this town seems to be interested in! Let's all overlook the fact that I am currently expertly organizing over six thousand square feet of historical treasures ranging from the Paleolithic Age to the Renaissance in this very building for your viewing and educational pleasure. That's all ancient history as far as anyone in this town is concerned! No, let's dig deeper into the day's worthless gossip instead!" Then getting his first good look at Carter he screeched, "What is that *abominable* creature?!"

"That's, uh, Carter. He's my pet."

To really paint the picture for him, I patted the chupacabra's furry head, but apparently my brushstrokes could've used a little work, because the dude still shrieked, "Pet *what*? SABERTOOTH?!"

"He's actually a rare species of canine," I said, figuring someone as snooty as him might like that. "Very rare, and from an *extremely* old bloodline."

Carter offered the curator his least fangy smile. Which, unfortunately, still contained an awful lot of fanginess.

"The creature looks positively *vampiric*!" he cried. "I haven't seen fangs like that since the last time we showcased our *Predators of the Ice Age* exhibit two years ago!"

Well, he wasn't so wrong about the predator part.

"Listen, we just have a couple of questions about what happened that night," I said, trying to steer this conversation away from our bloodsucking compadre and back to *Ernie's* padre. "We just wanted to hear how it all went down. You know, from the source."

"I've already given my statement to the press and the local law enforcement, and I'm sure you will find their communications more than satisfactory."

"I'm sure we would," Liza replied very diplomatically. "Only we're more interested in other stuff. Like, stuff you might not have told the papers or the police."

His cold green eyes were steady, but I thought I saw a flicker of unease sweep across the rest of his face. "What is this? What game are you three playing? Tween detective? What on earth would I be keeping from the police?"

Liza shrugged. "Maybe just something you thought wasn't important enough to mention, but might have struck you as a tad unusual."

"*Unusual?* I was clobbered on the head by a mallet and rendered unconscious for nearly two whole minutes! I'd say that is extremely unusual for someone in my line of work, wouldn't you agree? My, children are becoming increasingly *fish-brained* nowadays!"

"Could you give us a few more specifics, maybe?" I tried.

With a sigh dramatic enough to win him an Oscar (or at the very least a nomination), he sucked in a breath and started talking like someone who was giving the same tired speech for about the millionth time. "I received a phone call from Mr. Nez. He asked me if I was busy and if he could come meet with me in the museum. I told him that I was in fact busy, but that he could come over anyway, being our gracious sponsor and whatnot. He arrived promptly and eventually our conversation found its way to where it *always* does: the *El Dorado* exhibit. More specifically, he wanted to know if I'd changed my mind, if I would allow him to personally examine the three artifacts—the dagger, the sombrero, and the witch's riddle—with some new techniques he'd recently discovered. Naturally, I told him what I've been telling him for a Jurassic Age—that there are no hidden markings or symbols on any of the artifacts. Nevertheless, he continued to press the matter, and the conversation quickly deteriorated into an argument, whereupon he walked away with smoke practically billowing from his ears. Then, moments later, while I was distracted in this very office, he snuck up behind me and clonked me on the head with what must've been a chef's meat mallet! When I came to, I immediately contacted the police. But by that time, the filthy scoundrel had already run off with the artifacts. And that's really all there is to it."

"My dad is *not* a filthy scoundrel," Ernie growled, his dark eyes blazing with anger.

"Ah, so you're the spawn of that cowardly thief!" spat the curator.

"Hey, cool it with the name-calling, Teddy Roosevelt," I said.

Ira Baddensworth's pinched little eyes glared around at us like we were four greasy fingerprints on one of his priceless vases. "My, you strike me as a snoopy bunch. Let me give you three a valuable piece of advice my mother once gave me: don't stick your noses in drawers where they don't belong, because one day they might get slammed shut on you!"

Suddenly something the curator had said a few seconds ago sort of bubbled to the surface of my brain. "Hold up," I jumped in. "Did you say you were hit on the head with 'what must've been a chef's meat mallet'? Meaning, you didn't actually *see* Mr. Nez hit you?"

"I didn't need to *see* him hit me!" the curator sneered at me through clenched teeth. "Just like I didn't need to *see* him steal those artifacts! The night watchmen had already made their rounds and locked all the doors. I personally let Mr. Nez in through the main entrance. That two-bit crook was the only other body—warm body, at least; there is a mummy exhibit on the second floor—in this entire building! The security cameras established that fact!"

"But you told the police you saw him hit you," Liza pointed out.

"Maybe I did. So what?! He *did* hit me!"

"But if you didn't see him do it, then you can't be one hundred percent sure!" I shouted.

"Oh, but I can! I can be one *million* percent sure!"

At that moment, one of the museum staff tapped

the curator warily on the shoulder, the way he might've tapped a sleeping grizzly bear. "Pardon me, curator; there are two detectives waiting to speak with you."

He pointed the antenna of his walkie-talkie back toward the entrance of the civic center, and I spotted the pair of detectives he was talking about.

"I believe this concludes our little meeting here," Ira snapped at us. "Now, *scram*! And take that scraggly, sorry excuse for a dog with you!"

CHAPTER 7

"You were right!" I told Ernie as the four of us hopped down the steps of the civic center into the bright, hot sunshine. "The curator *was* lying! But not only was he lying, I bet you *he's* the villain! Heck, I'd even bet the Babe Ruth rookie card that I totally don't own on it!"

Liza gave me one of her classic *Jorge, gimme a break* looks.

"I mean it!" I said. "Haven't you ever watched *NCIS: Los Angeles*? It's a frame job! The curator's behind the whole thing! The guy's a snake in the grass!"

"*SNAKES?*" Carter shrieked, whirling around like a dog chasing its own tail. "WHERE? I hate snakes!"

"Easy there, big guy. It's just an expression."

"You really believe that, Jorge?" Ernie asked me, his brown eyes suddenly full of a sort of desperate hope. "You think that creep's trying to frame my dad?"

"Like a portrait! Let's examine all the facts. Fact número uno: that slimeball of a curator is the only eyewitness to the crime and he *barely* witnessed anything! Fact number two: he conveniently forgot to tell the police that he didn't actually *see* your dad hit him. And fact number three: he's a dead ringer for this two-faced used-car salesman guy I saw in an episode of *NCIS* last year! That's got to count for something, no?"

Somehow Liza still looked skeptical. "So, what? You're suggesting he stole the artifacts himself?"

"Why not?" I said. "It's not impossible. Heck, maybe Ernie and his dad are right! Maybe there really is some secret info on those museum pieces. And maybe that info really does lead to El Dorado! And maybe the curator realized it and is now trying to frame the only other person who knows about it, so he can keep the treasure all for himself!"

"You can make a bowl of maybe soup with all those maybes, Jorge." So Liza wasn't buying it. But at least Carter seemed to be smelling what I was cooking.

"What a sneaky sneak, dat guy!" he growled, turning back toward the civic center and bearing his fangs. "I go back in there right now and fang him in the butt! I gon' suck all his blood!"

"Whoa, whoa, easy there, Count Dracula," said Liza, taking Carter's leash from Ernie and tugging on it to make him follow as the three of us continued down the sidewalk beneath the shade of the pecan trees that lined the avenue. "We haven't proved anything yet. It's just an interesting hypothesis at the moment."

"I'm with Jorge!" Ernie announced. "I mean, why

else would that creep be making up these stories about my dad?!"

Even though Liza didn't seem fully on board with my theory just yet, she at least appeared to be toying with it now, like a cat pawing at an interesting ball of yarn. "It's kind of a stretch... but I guess it *is* possible."

"C'mon, Liza, deep down inside you know I'm right," I said. "So what do we do? How do we catch this guy? You're the brains of the operation!"

Carter frowned, confused. "If she da brains, then what am I?"

Ernie, who happened to be staring into one of Carter's long, fur-tipped *orejas*, said, "You're the eyes... and the, uh, *ears*."

Liza paused for a sec, thinking. "Look, none of us actually believe that slimy curator. That's a given. But if we're going to get the police on our side, we need *evidence*. What we need is another eyewitness."

CHAPTER 8

A second eyewitness.

That's what this whole case was going to boil down to. If we wanted to clear Ernie's dad's name, then we were going to have to find somebody who could contradict the curator's story. And the logical place to begin our search was with the neighbors.

The civic center sat right in the middle of a nice, quiet neighborhood in central Boca Falls, surrounded by about fifty houses and two big apartment complexes that had a direct view of the center. But the whole "knocking on doors and asking questions" thing was way harder than those TV detective shows made it look. First off, a lot of people wouldn't even open their doors to us.

Right off the bat I realized we were going to need some kind of angle. And that's when I came up with another brilliant idea!

Since Carter was the scariest-looking member of our gang, I figured he should wear the Girl Scout costume. All we had to do was buy about thirty boxes of cookies from a *real* Girl Scout, and we were in business!

My scheme worked surprisingly well, actually. Doors opened, people bought cookies, Carter got a handful of funny looks, and we got to ask our questions.

Problem was, everyone we talked to basically said the same thing: the people who had heard the screams hadn't seen anything, and the ones who hadn't heard them had been asleep or away. Not one person had seen or heard anything that they hadn't already reported to the police.

And surprise, surprise, we soon realized we weren't the only ones canvassing the neighborhood for other witnesses.

On two different occasions, we spotted the trench coat–wearing detective duo from the civic center knocking on doors and taking notes.

Anyway, once we'd exhausted our supply of doors to knock on (and our supply of Girl Scout cookies), we decided to hit the local dog park, which was about five blocks east of the civic center and was popular with the neighborhood.

Things actually started off pretty well there—lots of people told us what they'd heard (always describing the same piercing, bloodcurdling scream) and told us that they'd ask friends to see if maybe they had seen something suspicious. But then this overgrown poodle started sniffing Carter's rear end, and things suddenly took a turn for the—well, *wild*...

At any rate, after close to ten straight hours of hardcore gumshoeing, I was starting to feel a little exhausted. My feet hurt from too much walking, my tummy hurt from sneaking too many Thin Mints, and my vocal cords hurt from asking too many questions like "So, did you or your cats see anything odd that night?" I was honestly starting to feel a little sorry for myself.

But the person I was feeling sorriest for was Mr. Nez. The truth was, we were probably the only people in town out here trying to prove his innocence.

And we were getting absolutely nowhere. Even worse, what if the man really was innocent? I mean, can you imagine getting into huge trouble for something you didn't even do? The sad part was that I actually could.

Once, back home in L.A. when my mom and I were living over in Huntington Park, I almost got arrested for shoplifting. It was nuts. I was playing basketball with my friends on a public court across the street from this line of bodegas and shops, and this cop comes over and tells me to show him my bookbag. Then he starts poking around in my stuff, dumping my things all over the place, and even pats me down right there in front of a bunch of kids from my neighborhood, like I was some kind of criminal.

The cop even called my mom and it turned into this huge show with about fifty people watching from the sidewalks. Apparently a kid in the neighborhood had stolen something expensive from one of the shops across the street. I guess the kid looked sort of like me, and that's how the whole thing started.

The point is, I felt totally and completely humiliated. Totally and completely powerless. Even though I was *innocent*. Even though I hadn't done a single thing wrong!

I can't describe what an awful feeling that is, and I couldn't help but wonder if that's exactly how Ernie's dad was feeling right now. Just the thought made me sick to my stomach, like I'd eaten a bad gas-station enchilada.

But the worst part? We were about as close to solving this case as Carter was to swearing off blood and becoming a fruitarian.

Translation: not close at *all*. The four of us were fresh out of ideas and nowhere even near finding a counter-eyewitness.

Fortunately, an eyewitness would soon find *us*...

CHAPTER 9

It was a couple of minutes after 7:00 and I had just come in from walking Liza home when the phone rang.

"Hello?" I said, picking it up.

"Dude, what's your problem?" I screamed back. "You could've busted my eardrum!"

"Perdón, perdón," came a small, nervous voice

from the other end. It sounded like an older boy or a young man. "But I—I need help. Can you lend me a hand?"

"Buddy, I can lend you my whole fist," I said, balling up the fingers of my free hand. "Just let me know where you're at."

"I'm still at the civic center."

I blinked. The civic center? "Hey, who is this?"

Silence. Then: "Can you help me?"

"Can I help you with *what*? Who is this?"

"The newspapers got the story all wrong," said the mystery voice. "They're crumpling the wrong man's brim. Come find me if you want the truth."

"What story? Are you talking about the museum robbery?"

"What else? I'll be waiting outside. But you have to hurry before *they* find me!"

Click!

Suddenly, the line went dead. But just as suddenly, our chances of busting this case wide-open were looking very much alive!

CHAPTER 10

"I don't get how we're supposed to find him..." Liza whispered as the four of us crept sneakily around the side of the civic center exactly forty-five minutes later. "Especially when we don't even know what he looks like!"

Carter frowned. "He didn't tell you what he look like, Jorge?"

"Didn't say where we should meet him, either," Liza pitched in.

"Because he couldn't!" I tried to explain for the gazillionth time. "He's obviously in some kind of danger. But he's got to be around here. Somewhere."

"I don't like this, guys." Ernie's dark eyes were darting anxiously around the gloom. "Anyone remember what happened in the *Star Trek* episode 'Day of the Dove'?"

"No!" Liza and I snapped in unison.

E-dog sighed disappointedly at our lack of Star Trek nerdiness, giving us a *Do you two live under a rock?* type of pitying look. "Well, that's the one when Captain Kirk gets lured into a trap on planet Beta XII-A by a noncorporeal alien entity. And that's EXACTLY what this smells like!"

"I jess smell cabra," said Carter with a hungry lick of his lips.

I grinned at the Hungry Hungry Hippo. "Dude, are you always thinking about goats?"

Pearly white fangs gleamed dangerously in the moonlight as the chupacabra returned my grin. "Not always. Jess most of the time."

Liza rolled her eyes. "Can we focus on the mission instead of goats?" she whispered.

As we went slinking all ninja-like around to the back of the building, a sudden and horrible scream ripped the night in two!

Startled out of our socks—and pretty much everything *else* we were wearing—the four of us basically jumped into each other's arms in an überembarrassing group hug!

"More like, *who* was that?!" I corrected, my jacked-wide eyes frantically trying to scan in every direction at once.

"Who's there?" demanded Liza. "Who screamed?"

"It was me!" answered a voice from somewhere close by—a voice I recognized. The mystery caller! "Why'd you sneak up on me like that?! You could've made me snap my chin strap!"

"Sneak up on you?!" I screeched. "We can't even see you!"

"WHERE IS HE?" Ernie shrieked, looking around

in a panic. "I DON'T SEE HIM! HE MUST HAVE ACQUIRED A ROMULAN CLOAKING DEVICE!"

Fortunately for us, there was no alien technology in the Star Trek universe that could hide someone from Carter's bloodhound schnoz. A few quick sniffs at the balmy air was all it took.

"Da voice come from in there!" Carter hissed, swinging his head around and pointing, bird-dog style, at the thick clump of bushes growing wild along the side of the building. "And there's a goat in there, too!"

The chivo-slurping chupacabra made it about a half step toward the bushes when the voice cried, "No! Stay back! I have to know I can trust you before I reveal myself!"

Immediately my fingers closed around Carter's skinny wrist, and I yanked him back. "Dude, you're going to scare the living daylights out of him! Stay here."

"Trust *us*?" Liza shouted at the voice in disbelief. "We don't even know if we can trust *you*! Who are you?"

"He's the one who called me," I told her. "I recognize his voice!"

"You have a good ear," replied the mystery man. "A substantially oversized coco, but nonetheless a good ear."

Hold up. Did Mr. I'm Too Scared to Come Out of the Bushes just make a joke about the size of my head? Seriously?

Liza took a cautious step toward the shadowy bushes. "You still haven't told us who you are," she pointed out.

"And you still haven't told us how you got my number!" I snapped. Yeah, I was still a little sore over that completely uncalled-for dig at my cabeza.

"It was on a note," answered the voice. "On the curator's desk. It said: 'Trusty handyman.'"

Trusty handyman? What was he talking ab—

Oh! Of course! I slapped my forehead. *¡Mi abuelo!*

My grandpa had been helping out at the civic center as a handyman when the museum peeps first started setting up. The curator had probably kept his number *handy* in case they needed help with a lighting installation or something.

"Jorge, I not messin'!" The chupacabra tugged anxiously on my arm, like a first grader who really needed to pee. "There really is a chivo in there!"

"You need to get a grip," I told the thirsty bloodsucker. "And loosen the one on my arm before I can't feel my fingers anymore!"

"But I can smell it, Jorge! I can smell it! *Issa old goat in there!*" Ever tried to stop a hungry Sasquatch from cutting in line at an IHOP all-you-can-eat buffet? Well, it was kind of like that.

"You said you had information about the museum robbery," Ernie said to the bushes. "What do you know?"

"Plenty!" the voice answered. "But this isn't the time or place to play twenty questions. I'm up to my crown in danger! I just barely managed to escape the museum by the skin of my brim!"

Liza's mouth curved down in a worried frown. "What kind of danger are you in?"

Finally, Carter's self-control meter blew a gasket. "THERE'S A GOAT IN THERE, JORGE!" he cried. "¡UN CHIVO! *¡UN CHIIIIIIVO!*"

Then, shrugging me off like a leaf, he charged the bushes in what can only be described as a bloodthirsty frenzy! Fangs out, deadly razor-sharp claws gleaming dangerously in the moonlight!

CHUPACARTER AND THE SCREAMING SOMBRERO

"He . . . *gone!*" gasped Carter, big eyes bugging with bewilderment. "Jess left his hat! An old goatskin hat! Dat's why I smelled old goat!"

"And *I* smell an ignoramus!" barked an annoyed disembodied voice.

For a dizzy second, I had no idea where it could have possibly come from. But then my eyes nearly bugged out of my face as I realized there was only *one* possibility!

It was the hat.

The sombrero.

The thing had *talked*!

CHAPTER 11

I gaped, my eyes feeling about a millimeter away from popping out of their sockets. "But you're . . . a hat!"

"Who were you expecting?" the sombrero clapped back. "Yoda?"

I felt like I'd taken a long trip with Alice down the rabbit hole. The world wobbled around me. Reality had apparently taken a lunch break.

"I—I don't get it..." I whispered.

"Give it your best shot," urged the sombrero, so I did.

"You're a *sombrero*?"

"So far, so good."

"A sombrero that... *talks*?"

"Right again."

"You—you're a *talking sombrero*?"

"Three for three, big guy! My, you are a smart one! Now, is there anything not completely and *painfully* obvious that any of you would like to contribute to this conversation?"

"Issa talking sombrero!" Carter gasped, as if the whole ridiculous situation had finally dawned on him.

"Oh, brother... a whole gang of geniuses." The hat—or I guess, *he*—let out a tired groan. "No matter. Which one of you is the trusty handyman?"

"Huh?" one of us managed.

"The handyman! I need a *handyman*!"

"What could you possibly need a handyman for?" asked Liza.

"Isn't it obvious?" erupted Señor Sombrero. "I need a man with *hands*—a *hand*yman—who I can trust to pick me up and get me out of here! Do you have any idea how hard it is to wobble around everywhere on the edges of your brim?" And when we all sort of paused to think about it for a second, he exploded, "No! Of course you don't! Because none of you are sombreros! Now stop wasting time!"

All of a sudden a wedge of yellow light sliced through the darkness on this side of the civic center.

"I smell Doritos!" whispered Carter, sniffing the air. "The security guard comin'!"

We all gulped. "C'mon! ¡Vámonos!" hissed the hat urgently, and he didn't need to tell us twice.

I tossed Mr. Sombrero over to Carter for safekeeping (well, mostly because I was still too terrified to actually hold the thing), and the four of us ran like our sneakers had suddenly caught candela.

CHAPTER 12

"What's wrong with you people?" snapped the ticked-off fashion accessory. "Never seen a handsome handmade sombrero before?!"

"Not one with as big a mouth as yours," I said. "That's for sure."

CHUPACARTER AND THE SCREAMING SOMBRERO

And no joke, the sombrero stuck his tongue out at me! It was way longer and way more pinkish than you'd expect a sombrero's tongue to be. Especially if you're anything like me and didn't expect a sombrero to have a tongue in the first place.

"That thing's not gonna suck my blood, is it?" the hat asked uneasily, and somehow Carter's expression became even more shocked.

"You got blood?" he whispered.

"No. But if I did, would you try to suck some?"

The chupacabra thought deeply about that for a second. "Maybe just a sip?"

And suddenly—

"THE MONSTER WANTS TO DRINK MY BLOOD!" shrieked the sombrero.

"Dude, turn the volume down about fifty notches!" I whisper-raged. "My grandma is only two rooms over! And if you get her upset, you're going to see a *real* monster!"

"Oye, keep Mr. Fangs away from me!" cried the hat, making a wobbling retreat toward the far corner of my desk.

"Relax! He's not going to bite you."

"You better not be lying to me, cabezón!"

"You keep making jokes about my head, *I'm* the one who's going to bite you!"

"Don't take this the wrong way," Liza said to Señor Bigmouth. "I'm speaking strictly as a woman of science, but—*how do you exist?!*"

The sombrero looked pretty annoyed at her question. Well, as annoyed as a goat-leather shade provider can look. "What kind of question is that? You don't hear me asking how your fang-toothed abomination over there exists!"

"Yeah, but at least it's not that hard to imagine how something like him *could* possibly exist," Liza countered. "He clearly falls somewhere in the kingdom of animalia—albeit a really *strange* section of that kingdom. But you're a *hat*. That speaks English."

"So what if I speak English?" the sombrero shot back. "I also speak Nahuatl. And Spanish. And Portuguese, too! I've spent the last *thousand years* traveling this world from museum to museum, and you find it odd that I would've learned a language or two? *Pffft!*"

"But how do you produce sound with your mouth?" Liza pressed. "How do you even *HAVE* a mouth?"

"I have an idea!" the sombrero said, sounding almost cheery all of a sudden. "Why doesn't everybody just sit down and get comfy, and I'll tell you my whole life story. How's that? Sound good?"

"Sounds awesome!" Ernie dropped excitedly to the floor in the middle of my room. "Go ahead! We're listening."

"NO! DON'T SIT! DON'T GET COMFY!" the hat roared at him. "This isn't story time! Can't any of you get this through your thick skulls? I'm being hunted!"

"Hunted by who?" I shouted.

"By the thieves who robbed the museum! Who else, junior Einstein?"

"Hold on—did you just say 'thieves'?" asked Liza, surprised. "Meaning, more than one?"

If hats could glare, this one definitely glared at her. "Of course I meant more than one! What do you think the *s* at the end of a noun is there for? Decoration?!"

"Wait. Did you actually see them? Like, with your own"— I didn't see any eyes on the guy, so I went with—"*whatevers*?"

"Listen to this brainiac! If I didn't see them, how would I know they were there?"

"Maybe you heard them with your"—I didn't see any ears on the guy either, so again I went with—"*whatevers*?"

The hat shook his brim in outrage. "Unbelievable. You'd think with *all* that head, you'd at least have a *bit* of brains in there somewhere."

¡Cielos! What a mouth on this guy! Who knew a piece of headwear could have such an obnoxious personality?

"Well, what'd the thieves look like?" asked Liza.

"They wore masks, so I couldn't see their faces," said the sombrero. "But one was very tall and skinny and the other two were very thick and short."

"That proves it right there!" shouted Ernie, leaping up with a rush of excitement. "That proves my dad is innocent!"

CHAPTER 13

Anyone who had ever seen Ernie's dad could tell you with 100 percent certainty that Mr. Nez, standing at a towering six foot four and with the rough dimensions of an NFL lineman, didn't even come close to fitting the description of the museum thieves provided by Señor Sombrero. Mr. Nez wasn't skinny and he definitely wasn't short. He was both *very* tall and *very* thick, built like your average grizzly bear. He also hadn't been wearing any kind of mask. The security cameras proved that much. So if the sombrero was to be believed (and there was no reason *not* to believe him), then Ernie's dad really was innocent!

"So tell us what happened!" I said to the hat as relief crashed over me like a waterfall. "How'd it go down? The robbery, I mean."

"To be honest, it started off like any other day," he confided. "As the crown jewel of the Museum of Natural Wonders, I spent the morning being pampered by my loyal staff. I received a careful dusting, a thorough oiling, followed next by a light polishing, as is my monthly ritual. Then, for the next few hours, I dazzled and enchanted some of Curator Ira's close friends, whom he'd brought in for a private peek at me. One man in particular I liked very much. He knew quite a lot about my history and went on and on about what a magnificent and priceless piece I was. You could tell he has an *excellent* eye for quality. His name was Mr. Nez, I believe. I tend to remember classy characters like that."

"Mr. Nez?" Ernie gasped. "Are you serious?"

"Of course I'm serious. Why would I make this up?"

"And was he wearing a big green bow tie?"

"In fact, he was wearing a big green bow tie." The sombrero sounded surprised. "How did you know that?"

"Because that was my dad!" Ernie explained. Then, turning to Liza and me: "That's his lucky bow tie! He thought it might help him when he went to talk to the curator."

"What happened next?" Liza wanted to know.

The sombrero continued. "For a long while, nothing. Most of Ira's friends left, and at around nine o'clock the security guard made his final rounds and locked all the doors from the outside. Only Ira and the man with the bow tie were still inside—both in Ira's office, just off the main exhibit hall."

"And where were you?"

"As chance would have it, I was on a table off to the side in the main hall. Ira had been showing me off to the bow tie man and had yet to return me to the protective glass case along with the other *El Dorado* exhibit pieces—the dagger and the riddle."

"What happened next?"

"That's when they began to argue. Ira and this Mr. Nez. They began shouting at one another. I honestly couldn't make out very much of what they were saying. But a few moments later, the bow tie man went storming out of the office, passing through the principal exhibit area on his way out the front door, which he didn't even bother shutting behind himself. And *that's* when I saw them!"

"Saw who?"

"The thieves! ¡Los ladrones! They had slipped silently into the main hall and were lurking in deep shadows. They were clearly experts—professional thieves! You could tell by the way they moved, silent as ghosts, and the way they communicated to each other, using only the subtlest of hand movements. I watched with unspeakable horror as one of the three snuck up behind Ira in his office and with a single vicious blow knocked him unconscious!"

The sombrero cleared his . . . throat? "Nothing. Perdónenme. I just got caught up in my own story and scared myself."

Liza and I looked at each other and just shook our heads. This guy—er, *hat*—was really something.

"My name is Enrique, by the way," the hat informed us. "Nice to meet all of you."

We all introduced ourselves, too—you know, to be polite. Then Liza said: "You were telling us about the heist..."

"Ah, ¡sí! Well, almost at that very moment, mere *seconds* after the thieves knocked Ira unconscious, the green bow tie man came back in through the front door, saying something about having forgotten his briefcase and some not-so-nice things about Ira. He found the briefcase on a table near the entrance and then went quickly out again. But the instant he was gone, the thieves began ransacking the *El Dorado* exhibit! They broke into the display case, took the dagger and la bruja's riddle, and threw them into a backpack."

"And they didn't scream?" I asked.

The sombrero—or, Enrique, I guess—hesitated.

"Are you talking about the other exhibit pieces?"

"Yeah. I'm assuming they can talk, too, right?"

"Oh, *of course* they talk," replied Enrique. "In fact, the three of us regularly discuss all kinds of things. Music, food, the latest fashion trends. NO! Of course they can't talk, you seaweed brain! They're inanimate objects! Why would you assume they *talk*? ¡Estás frito! 'They can talk'!"

Yep. I had just received a wicked tongue-lashing from a furious talking hat. And my mom had sent me out here from L.A. so I could have a "normal life." Go figure.

"Where was I?" the sombrero went on. "Ah, yes. At that point, I was quaking with fear! I could hardly keep my chin strap from trembling! But it wasn't long before the thieves realized that I, the most important piece of the most important exhibit in the entire museum—and likely, the entire *world*—was missing from the display case. I knew they would stop at nothing to find me! Who could blame them? And so in my terror I began to scream! I screamed and screamed, as loud as I could—and it worked! The thieves panicked! They had no idea who or where the screams were coming from."

"That must've been the screaming that the neighbors heard!" Liza said excitedly, just as it dawned on me, too.

"Then, just seconds later," continued Enrique, "by some miracle, Ira regained consciousness. I saw him pick up the phone and dial for help! The thieves must've heard him as well, because they quickly fled the exhibit area, and that was the last I saw of them. Naturally, I took the first opportunity, which would come a day later, to escape, knowing the thieves would most certainly be back for me at some point—and that I was nothing more than a sitting hat in the museum!"

"I think the expression is actually 'a sitting duck,'" Ernie corrected.

"¿A duck?" Enrique spat in disbelief. "Take a good look at me! Do I quack? Do I have big flappy wings and feathers?! I'm a sombrero! Why on earth would I be a sitting *duck*?!"

"Hey, duck, hat—who cares?!" I cheered. "You're exactly what we've been looking for!"

CHAPTER 14

As weird as it's going to sound, we spent the next ten minutes bringing the sombrero up to speed. We told him all about how one of his favorite people in the world, "Mr. Green Bow Tie Man"—aka Ernie's dad—was currently behind bars, accused of assault and of stealing the exhibit pieces. Then I started telling the gang how now that we knew the truth, we could go straight to the authorities, explain everything! But that was right about when Liza decided it was time to pop the balloon of my enthusiasm with her logic pin.

"And by 'everything,' you mean what, exactly?" she said. "That a *talking sombrero* told us Ernie's dad didn't rob the exhibit? That the same *talking sombrero* says it was really three professional thieves?"

"Why do you keep emphasizing the 'talking sombrero' part?" the talking sombrero wanted to know.

"Because that's the part no cop on the face of this planet is going to believe!" Liza snapped.

It was a fair point. "They don't have to believe us, Liza! He can tell the police himself!"

"Ha! You take me anywhere *near* a police station and I'll zip up tighter than a Ziploc bag!" spat Enrique. "I won't say a word. ¿Me oíste?"

"Why not?!"

"Because I'm not talking to anybody I don't have to! Don't you understand? My life is on the line! ¡Mi vida! And that's all that matters to me in this world—*me*! My favorite number is número uno, and that's as high as I ever aim to count! Think about it: If you take me to the police, they'll simply hand me right back to the museum, and then the thieves will know exactly where I am and they'll try to kidnap me again! It would defeat the whole point of me escaping!" The self-centered chatterhat gave the circle of his brim a furious shake, like a dog trying to shake off water after a bath. "Besides, I don't like talking to people! Most of the time they just faint. It's super annoying, and that's why I have my golden rule: never talk to anybody I don't trust! You four are the only people in the world right now who know I'm not your average exceedingly *beautiful*, exceedingly *precious* piece of headwear. And you've got to protect me. ¡Por Dios! You got to keep me safe from those robbers!"

"You really have to pull yourself together," I told him. "You don't even know they're still after you. I mean, why would they want you so bad?"

"Because *he's* the missing piece . . ." whispered Ernie. The way he said it was like in a movie when someone realizes something super important. It kind of gave me goose bumps. "Don't you get it, Jorge? These thieves are probably treasure hunters, and like any good treasure hunter, they know the legends back to front! They know they need *all* three pieces the witch left behind in order to discover the secret location of El Dorado!"

For the first time all night, the sombrero actually sounded impressed with one of us. "¡Eso! And how do you know so much about the legend?"

The grin that split Ernie's lips was a big one. "My dad and I are big fans."

"Aha! So that's how you can talk!" I said to the hat. "The bruja! The one from the El Dorado myth!

She must've accidently enchanted one of her dusty old sombreros!"

Mr. Short, Tan, and Leathery clearly didn't like that. "Who you calling old and dusty, pumpkin-head?"

"Am I right, though? The witch did this to you. She waved her magic broom and *wham!* A magical talking sombrero. Am I close?"

The next ten seconds marked the longest stretch of time that Motor Mouth over here had ever shut up for as long as we'd known him. When he finally spoke again, his voice was hardly more than a whisper. "Sí, something like that..."

"Okay, so if you're supposed to be one of la bruja's clues, then where's the treasure?" I picked up the sombrero, checking on the underside of his brim for a treasure map, but didn't see one. "Nothing under here."

"¡Oye! ¡No me toques! NO. ME. *¡TOQUES!*" he snapped, flapping angrily in my hands. "Didn't you hear what your buddy just told you?! You need ALL three clues to discover the location of El Dorado! I'm just your everyday magical talking hat! What do I know about hidden treasure?!"

"Guys, you know what this means, don't you?"

said Liza, suddenly sounding very serious. "If the hat from the legend is real (and he looks pretty real to me), that means the witch from the legend must be real, too. And if *she's* real, then the *treasure* is real."

Throwing his hands up, Ernie let out the loudest, most annoyed sigh you ever heard. "Of course the treasure's real, Liza! I've been telling you that for months."

"Actually, that doesn't even matter," Liza continued. "All that matters is that those thieves believe it's real. Think about it: they didn't steal a single thing from any other exhibit—just the *El Dorado* stuff. They're obviously after the treasure!"

"What's your point?" asked Ernie.

"My point is that the sombrero is the last piece of the puzzle, and those villains aren't going to stop until they've got him. Which means he really is in danger!"

"I tip my sombrero to you!" shouted Enrique. "Thank you! At least someone here gets it."

"I'm not risking my neck for some bigmouthed fashion accessory," I told Liza. "What's one hat's life really worth, anyway?

She gave me a disappointed look. "Every life is precious, Jorge."

"Even his?"

"Especially mine!" snapped the hat.

Liza ignored me. She said, "What we have to do is find a way into the museum."

A look of confusion wrinkled Carter's furry face. "The front doors no work?"

"I mean, a sneaky way into the museum."

Yeah, she'd totally lost me, too. "Liza, what are you talking about?"

"That's the only way we're going to be able to prove Mr. Nez's innocence!" she explained. "We have to find some rock-solid, incontrovertible proof that those three thieves were actually in the civic center that night and that they, and not Ernie's dad, are the real thieves. We're going to have to bust in."

"Wait. So you're saying we have to commit a crime in order to prove that my dad *didn't* commit a crime?" Ernie sounded like he was having a tough time following Liza down this particular logic trail.

Liza shrugged. "Pretty much."

"But we can't break into a museum!" I told her. "That's almost impossible! We're not professional cat burglars!"

"I didn't say it was going to be easy, Jorge. Especially not with how tight security is going to be after the robbery."

"We could always sneak in through the skylight," suggested Ernie. "That's how they do it in all the Mission: Impossible movies."

"Look around the room, Ernie. You see Tom Cruise anywhere? Plus, I don't even think the civic center has a skylight."

"It does," said Carter, who was currently snacking on a bag of tostones.

"Okay. Let's say it does. But it would be locked, anyway."

The chupacabra shook his head. "It's not."

Three pairs of surprised eyes fell on the giant, chip-crunching cryptid. "How do you know that?" asked Liza.

"I was jess up there last night," the chupacabra explained. "Moon watching. I saw it."

"Carter, why were you moon watching on the civic center roof last night?" I snapped.

"Chupacabras nocturnal!" he snapped back. "And you three lazies sleep all night long! I gotta do *some*thing..."

Eh. The overgrown mosquito had a point.

"Carter, back to the skylight," said Liza. "You're sure it's unlocked?"

He gave a quick nod. "I remember, 'cause I thought it was weird."

"Then why didn't you tell us before?" asked Ernie.

"'Cause I didn't think it was *that* weird. Oh, and I found these super-cool metal toothpicks!" He demonstrated, picking a chunk of deep-fried banana from between the rows of his gleaming white fangs.

"Carter, those aren't toothpicks!" exclaimed Liza, examining one. "Those are *lock*picks! The thieves must've used them to break in through the skylight!"

Ernie gave her a smug look. "I told you that was how all the pros do it!"

"That's why the curator never saw anyone else come in or out!" I shouted as all the puzzle pieces clicked gloriously into place for me. "That's why only Ernie's dad shows up on the security footage."

"Exactly!" A sly grin curled the corners of Liza's lips as she held up one of the lockpicks. "And now it's *our turn* to pay the museum an unexpected visit..."

CHAPTER 15

Going straight to the police with the lockpicks obviously wouldn't do us much good.

First of all, they wouldn't even take us seriously. Everyone in town knew that Ernie, Liza, and I were best buds, and they'd probably just figure it was some cockamamie scheme to save Mr. Nez's neck. Second, the police wouldn't ever be able to swipe a single print off the lockpicks (if there had been any to begin with), now that Carter's slobber was all over them. And lastly—but most problematically—if one of the detectives happened to mention our little theory to Ira the Wicked Curator of the West, you can be positively, no doubt, double-lock sure that he'd seal up the civic center skylight tighter than a can of sardines, and we'd lose our only way into the place. Plus, we could always hand the picks over to the cops after we'd unleashed our inner Spy Kids.

At any rate, the plan was now set! Tomorrow night, the three of us (along with our goat-skinned, loudmouthed compadre) were going to sneak into the civic center, search for any solid evidence pointing to the real thieves, and hope we didn't end up in handcuffs. It wasn't going to be easy. Especially the "not ending up in handcuffs" part. But nothing worth doing usually is.

The next morning, I woke up to, well—an *interesting* sight...

I'd heard video games were good for making friends, but I never thought a PlayStation could bring a chupacabra and a goatskin sombrero together. Guess you learn something new every day, huh?

The two of them were still button-mashing after I'd finished my breakfast and dressed for school, so I told them to sit tight and not to break anything while I was gone.

"You heard the kid, Furry," Enrique told Carter. "Behave yourself." Then, wobbling around on the edges of his brim to face me, he said: "Bueno, ¡vamos! Saddle me up and let's get galloping, cowboy!"

"Dude, I'm not wearing you to school," I told him.

"What? Why not?"

"'Cause I said so."

"But I'm a sombrero! I need to be in a hat box or *on* a head! It's the only way I feel . . ."

"Feel *what*?"

"Feel safe, okay? It's my natural habitat! I get anxious, and every hat deserves a warm place to sit. Please just let me wear you."

"That sounds wrong. And no, I'm not going to let you *wear* me." My gaze slid to Big C. "Carter, keep an eye on that—" I almost said "guy" but instead went with "head garage."

"You can't seriously leave me alone with that thing!" Enrique screeched.

"Why not? You were both just tag teaming on *Fortnite*. That makes you battle buddies!"

"But look at the way he looks at me!"

Eh. It *was* sort of creepy.

"Carter, stop looking at him like that!" I hissed.

"Sorry, Jorge! But he smell sooo good!"

"He smells like a musky old *hat*," I pointed out.

"Yeah, but with a delicious hint of free-range goat!"

"See what I mean?" yelled Enrique.

"Look, he's not going to *eat* you, okay?" Just to be sure, though, I glanced sideways at Carter to double-check. "Right?"

The chupacabra thought for a moment, then gave a very unconvincing nod. "Right."

"There, it's settled!" I said. "And did you ever stop to think about what would happen if someone saw me wearing you out in public and recognized you?" I asked the hat.

"Like who?" Enrique challenged.

"Like the curator, for one! He'll probably have me arrested on the spot!"

"Nobody's going to notice, chico. Check this out!"

Suddenly, the sombrero hunkered down and began making these weird grunting sounds, sort of like how weightlifters do when they're trying to lift the backside of a 747 over their heads in a strongman competition.

"Hey, take it easy!" I shouted. "You're gonna bust a stitch!" But that's not what happened. Instead the sombrero began to change! The tall pointy crown first popped straight up, like the tip of a paper party hat, then flattened way down as his wide goatskin brim stretched out even further and started curling up at the edges like an old photograph. Next thing I knew, his color had changed, too—going from a deep rusty brown to a light tan color bordering on peach!

"¡Ahí! ¿Ves? Now, tie that belt around me, would you?" he asked Carter, who looked like a five-year-old who had just witnessed his very first magic trick. "Gracias. See? I look like a totally different sombrero!"

He really did, too. It was sort of amazing, actually. He was basically like Mystique from X-Men! If she were a hat, I guess.

"Dude, that was incredible!" I shouted.

"¡Wacha! Nice, huh?"

"Hey, I'll admit it—that's a pretty neat trick!"

"It's not a trick," he said very seriously. "It's *a gift*."

"Yeah, well, maybe it is. But I'm still not wearing you."

"Why not?!"

"Because you're about two gallons too big and three decades out of style!"

"You saying I'm not fashion-forward enough for you?"

"I'm saying you're like a complete fashion *rewind*! No offense or anything, but you're totally uncool."

"Uncool? ¡Estás frito! I'm the coolest thing in this entire room—I'm the coolest thing in this *entire town*!"

"Good. In that case, keep my room nice and chilly for me. I'll be back when school's out."

"You open that door, I scream!" Enrique threatened me.

"Enrique, stop messing around!" I warned him. "I'm going to be late."

I gripped the knob but had barely cracked the door open when the sombrero let out a shriek loud enough to raise the dead. "AAAAAAAHHHHHHHH!"

I immediately shut us in again. "Hey! If my grandma comes in here with her chancla, somebody's in for a world of slipper-induced hurt!"

"Yeah, and that somebody is *you,* ese," Enrique pointed out.

Darn it! The hat was right! I mean, I'd blamed my misbehavior on a lot of far-fetched things over the years, but blaming a whole bunch of ear-busting screams on a talking sombrero was a bridge too far. Even for me.

"Looks like we got ourselves an old-fashioned Mexican standoff here, amigo," said the sombrero with a mocking grin plastered across that leathery goatskin face of his.

And it clearly wasn't a standoff that I was going win.

1886, here I come...

CHAPTER 16

If you thought for one second that Paz was the only person in town with a middle school sense of humor, think again. In fact, there were exactly 1,289 kids in my school. And *all* of them had a middle school sense of humor.

It probably ranked in my top five all-time most embarrassing school days. *Ever.* On the bright side, though, at least Mr. Bigmouth Sombrero managed to keep his big leathery mouth shut.

That is, at least up until lunch.

I was standing toward the front of the long messy line, waiting for Liza and Ernie to show for third period lunch, when out of nowhere, the biggest, meanest, most blockheaded bully on the face of the planet cut in front of me. (Hint: It was Zane Zagorski.)

The good news: Zane hadn't noticed me, which was how I preferred it. The bad news: Enrique had noticed *him.*

"Look at this joker wearing a baseball cap indoors," he sighed annoyedly, wiggling himself a little lower on my head. "And backward! What a buffoon!"

I couldn't argue with that. He seemed like he had Zane pretty much pegged. Still, I told the sombrero to stick a cork in it as the lunch lady handed both Zane and me lunch trays loaded with meat loaf, mashed potatoes, and a huge serving of green beans.

CHUPACARTER AND THE SCREAMING SOMBRERO

But what did Señor Blab Machine do? Why, he kept blabbing, of course!

"You don't wear a *mesh* cap inside. The only hats you wear indoors are genuine sombreros, because a) we are one hundred percent natural, b) we smell great, and c) we make you look *GOOD*!"

"Dude, please shut up already!" I begged, hiding my mouth with my hand as I pretended to rub something out of my eye. I was trying to be all sneaky about it, but several kids were already starting to stare. I could feel their curious eyes on me like a swarm of itty-bitty creepy-crawlies.

"I refuse to shut up!" Enrique snapped. "That guy is a walking fashion crime!" He wriggled himself a little lower on my head, half falling across my eyes now, and I had to shove him up just so I could see! "Ha! And look at the number on his T-shirt, number zero. Which is exactly how much style that kid has!"

Okay, I'm not going to lie—that one totally got me. I tried my absolute best to choke back my laugh, but it came bursting out of me all the same.

Unfortunately, Zane heard it, too. And unfortunately, he wasn't exactly laughing.

Enormous meaty shoulders slowly turned—*Did this guy ever stop growing? ¡Dios mío!*—and a huge, angry face glared menacingly down at me from his enormous height.

"What did you say?" he growled. Then, realizing it was me: "Oh, it's you, Spudz. Almost didn't recognize you beneath that *dead cow* on your head!"

Nearby, a couple of caveman jocks laughed at that. Zane followed it up with "Nice sombrero. Or, should I say, sombre-*no*!"

More caveman laughter. I sighed. To call these guys peanut brains would be an insult to the intelligence of legumes everywhere.

Meanwhile the king caveman was all smiles. "You know what? Today's your lucky day, ese. I'm not gonna make you pay for what you just said. See, 'cause the way I look at it, you walking around school the rest of the day with that leather umbrella on your head is punishment enough!"

Now I joined in on the chorus of chimp-ish giggling (mockingly, of course). But Zane didn't like that.

Glaring at me, he stole a sporkful of mashed potatoes from my tray and shoveled it into his grinning mouth.

"We got a big game today, and I need the extra carbohydrates. Besides, you wouldn't eat your own kind, would ya, Spudz? That's basically cannonballism!"

Yeah. He'd said "cannonballism." You couldn't make this stuff up.

Anyway, I had just opened my mouth to point out that the word he was looking for was probably "cannibalism," and that if the soccer team would consider taking up that ancient and time-honored tradition and start eating one another, our world would quickly become a much friendlier place.

But then I thought better of it. I just wanted to get through today attracting as little attention as possible. And a shove-fest with Zane and his squad of soccer-ball-kicking minions would be hugely counterproductive.

The second they'd all turned back around, Enrique whispered, "Okay, do it now!"

"Dude, shhh!"

"What are you *waiting* for?" he hissed down at me. "You've got a lunch tray right there! Smack him over the head with it!"

"I'm going to smack *you* over the head if you don't zip it!"

"How are you going to let him talk about you—and, more importantly, about *me*—that way? I'm a priceless piece of headwear!" The sombrero was all riled up now—I'm talking *legitly* heated—and his velvety inner brim was squeezing my head so hard it was beginning to cut off the blood flow. "Let me at him then! I'll show him who's the dead cow!"

Having had just about enough, I tore Enrique off my head and slammed him down on the aluminum counter where I slapped a hand over his "mouth."

The sombrero struggled for a few seconds, then

finally seemed to chill out. But next thing I knew, he dipped the edge of his smooth flat brim into the mound of mashed potatoes on my tray and flung a huge scoop of cheesy, buttery goodness straight up into the air like a stingray flinging sand. A moment later, the airborne potatoes landed with a wet *splat*!

Smack dab in the middle of Zane's ball cap!

Oh, crud...

I watched with a mix of amusement and horror as the goopy taters ran down the back of the modern-day caveman's hairy neck, and his ears turned a bright, furious red. He whipped around to give me a look that could've grilled jalapeños.

"It wasn't me!" I shouted, showing him my empty hands. "Seriously! It was the hat!"

No joke, Zane's entire face had morphed into what I can only describe as a trembling mask of rage. If he'd been a dog, they would've had him tested for rabies! "Feeling funny today, Mr. Potato Head?" he growled through clenched teeth.

And if you thought Enrique had a big mouth... well, hold my Pepsi. "It's kind of ironic that you of all people should be calling anyone Mr. Potato Head at the moment," I pointed out.

I couldn't help myself. The guy literally had warm mashed potato dripping down the sides of his head as he stood there!

At any rate, I don't want to get too much into what happened next, but I'll just leave you with this little nugget of wisdom: there's only one thing on this planet that spreads faster than a wildfire—and that, my friends, is a good old-fashioned food fight.

CHAPTER 17

Naturally, *I* got blamed for the food fight. In all fairness, Zane did, too. Our new principal, Ms. Rodriguez, only gave me a week's detention and sent us both home early, which I thought was pretty fair of her.

Anyway, my grandparents picked me up after lunch, and on the ride home, Paz wanted all the juicy deets.

"I heard you pied a kid in the face with a cupcake!" she said, practically beaming with excitement in the passenger's seat.

You'd think she lived for food fights or something. And who knows? Maybe she did. My abuela was cool like that.

"Gosh, I wish I could've been there! One question, though—why start a food fight with something as delicious as a cupcake? Why not a corn cake instead?"

I shrugged. "It was just what I had handy. But that's not how the food fight started. That was like halfway through, when some kid called Ernie 'the filthy cat burglar's son' or something like that."

He wasn't the only one, either. I'd thought I had it bad with all the sombrero jokes, but from first period on, kids were taking pokes at Ernie, calling his dad everything from the Boca Burglar to Sticky Fingers Nez. It was sad how mean we could be to each other. It's almost like we didn't realize we were all just one big family. And not even only us humans—I'm talking *every* living thing on this planet. That's something I'd learned from hanging out with Carter.

"And what about that bully who started it?" asked Paz. "How'd you handle him?"

I grinned. "With about a trayful of buttery mashed potatoes down the front of his shirt."

"That's my grandson!" Paz cheered, smacking her hands together in delight. If my grandma had a heart, I think it would've swelled with pride right about then.

"Paz! What kind of lesson are you trying to teach

him?" my grandpa grumbled from behind the wheel. "Jorge, listen closely to what I'm about to tell you: violence is never the answer. And especially not food-related violence. Repeat this with me: cupcakes are for eating, not for throwing."

"Yeah, I got you," I told my grandpa. I mean, it *was* true, after all. Violence was no bueno, and cupcakes tasted way better than they flew. You live, you learn, I guess.

All of a sudden, from two lanes over, a huge black SUV swerved in front of us, nearly sideswiping our pickup's crummy old bumper.

My abuelo, being a stickler for traffic laws, smashed his horn, and the driver of the SUV slowed a little, then smashed *his* horn while making some not-so-friendly hand gestures in my grandpa's general direction.

My abuelo's entire face instantly turned the color of a guajillo chile. "Oh, so you're a tough guy, eh?" he roared. "Let's pull over and see how tough you really are! Oye, I'm Mexican—we've produced over fifty world boxing champions in the last twenty years! And I was a contender in my day! ¡Un tremendo luchador!"

So much for violence never being the answer, huh?

CHAPTER 18

Between being forced to lug a five hundred-gallon sombrero around on my head all day, getting smacked in the face by some fourth-grader's baked Alaska, and watching my grandpa challenge a random stranger to a roadside boxing match, I was pretty sure I'd maxed out my daily quota of surprises.

Little did I know there was yet another *sorpresa* waiting for me back at the house.

The detective lady stooped by the driver's side window, flashing her badge at us. It was one of those quick, all-wrist moves like you see in the movies. "Hello, Mr. and Mrs. Lopez," she said. "I'm Special Agent Sophia and this is Special Agent John. We're sorry to show up unannounced like this, but I'm afraid it couldn't be helped."

"Say no more, officers," my grandma replied as we got out of the truck. "I'm embarrassed to admit that I know all too well why you're here." Then she grabbed me by the arm and dragged me in front of them. "It's my delinquent grandson, Jorge."

Delinquent grandson?! "Who you calling a delinquent?" I started to say, but Paz went on talking right over me.

"Now, I want you both to know that none of his behavior is *our* fault. We didn't raise him. He came to us this way. That's all his mother's doing. But we all do the best we can for the troubled youths in our life, don't we?"

Troubled youths? Seriously?

"I can't tell you how many times I've said, 'Georgy, Georgy, my beloved grandson, violence is not the answer!' But he simply doesn't listen, I'm sorry to say."

That was it. I couldn't take it anymore. The safety release valve on my Patience Meter had officially blown.

"¡Ándale! 'Violence is not the answer'?!" I shouted. "You were just cheering me on for hitting a kid in the face with a cupcake!"

"Listen to that awful temper . . ." my grandma said, shaking her head disappointedly. "Go ahead, officers—arrest him. That's why you're here."

Detective Sophia looked confused. "We're not here to arrest your grandson, ma'am . . . We're here about the museum robbery."

"The museum robbery?" choked Paz. "But you already caught the crook—Ernie's dad!"

"Grandma!" I snapped.

"What?" she snapped back. "It's true!"

"Please allow me to be a little more specific, Mrs. Lopez," said Detective Sophia. "We're here looking for information on one of the missing exhibit pieces—*the sombrero*."

CHAPTER 19

Five minutes later, I was sitting nervously in the living room in my grandpa's favorite recliner, while the pair of trench-coat-wearing detectives eyed me suspiciously from the love seat.

It was hard not to feel like I'd somehow wound up on the set of one of those TV cop shows. The only thing missing was the classic good-cop, bad-cop routine, though I wasn't sure exactly how these two would pull it off, because the big, beefy guy seemed like a man of few words. And by few, I mean *none*.

"We were hoping you could provide us with a little information, Jorge," said Detective Sophia, bringing out one of those handy detective writing pads. "As we understand it, you are good friends with Ernie Nez, the accused's son. Is that accurate?"

I gulped. "Yeah. Sure. We're buddies."

The big guy just stared at me.

Detective Sophia asked, "How does he seem to you lately?"

"Who, Ernie? Fine, I guess. Not as happy-go-lucky as usual, obviously, but he's got that whole thing with his dad going on."

The big guy kept on staring.

"Speaking of Mr. Nez," said Detective Sophia, "do you and Ernie ever talk about what he's being accused of, or about the robbery itself?"

"Not too much," I lied.

"Has he ever talked to you about the stolen museum pieces? Particularly the missing sombrero?"

At the mere mention of the word "sombrero," a hot, prickly sweat broke out on my chest and arms, and I had to clear my dry-as-a-desert throat before answering. "Uh, no . . ."

Then I noticed that Detective Sophia was looking curiously up at Enrique! She stared. I gulped.

"Say, that's an interesting-looking sombrero," she said after a few moments.

¡Dios mío! She's onto us!

Fight-or-flight instincts are an amazing thing. With the amount of panic-infused adrenaline that dumped into my bloodstream right then, I was surprised I didn't go jet-packing straight through the roof! "Yeah, I—I got this one at a swap meet," I lied. "Not bad for a five-spot, huh?"

All of a sudden, the detectives were whispering sneakily to each other. This was what I caught:

"... sort of the same shape..."

"... color's wrong..."

"... and the size."

"It was the cheapest old hat there!" I blurted, just trying to say something—anything!—to distract them. But right at that instant, the touchy old sombrero gave my head a painful squeeze! He obviously hadn't liked me calling him cheap. *Or* old. "Ow!"

Detective Sophia glanced back at me. "Pardon?"

"Nothing. Just wanted to say that I have *terrible* taste in hats. *Ow!*" Yeah, the sombrero had done it again!

"Something bothering you?" she asked me with a look of genuine concern.

You mean besides this *jerk* of a fashion accessory sitting on my head?! "No, I'm fine! Just a little headache."

Then, as the detectives went back to whispering,

I tore Squeezy McBrim off my head and stuffed him underneath the couch. Maybe a little time-out with all the dust mites down there would teach him a valuable lesson in manners. Plus, the less those two trench coats saw of him, the better.

Anyway, it seemed like a good idea. "Seemed" being the key word.

Totally panicking—honestly not even *thinking*—I shouted, "God bless you!" Then, when the two detectives turned to look suspiciously in my direction again, I quickly corrected that to: "I mean God bless *me* . . . It's a very echoey room, you see. And sometimes I get confused about who it was that sneezed. But it was definitely me."

Wow.

Talk about an all-time *terrible* lie.

But in my defense, this was a tough spot!

A moment later, Detective John pulled a small photograph from his pocket and held it out to me. It was a picture of Enrique—all oiled up and shiny, posing like some world-famous fashion model inside a glass display case.

"Have you ever seen a sombrero like this in your friend Ernie's house?" she asked, studying me with such intense concentration that I was half-terrified she might be able to read the truth right off my face.

I gulped for what felt like the hundredth time in the last sixty seconds.

"No . . ."

"Have you seen this sombrero or another like it anywhere at all?"

Sure, just under the couch!

"No . . ."

"You know, if someone did happen to see it lying around somewhere, there would be a *very* handsome reward for that person."

I shook my head. "A reward?"

"Five thousand dollars, I believe. That's what the museum is offering."

Right as she said that, Detective John scribbled something in his notepad. He tapped her on the shoulder and her eyes went to the pad.

And at the exact same moment, Enrique shouted, "*Five thousand dollars? Psshh! I'm priceless!*"

Two pairs of detective eyes swung back in my direction.

Sophia blinked. "What was that?" she said.

"Oh, uh—uh, I mean, I'm *speechless*!" I stammered, my heart feeling like it was about a centimeter away from punching its way through my rib cage. "Th-that's an awful lot of money."

"Of course, if someone was worried that their grandparents might end up keeping all the money," continued the detective lady, "we could always offer *other* rewards, such as super-wide flat-screen TVs with surround sound speaker systems."

CHUPACARTER AND THE SCREAMING SOMBRERO

My eyes drifted down to where I'd hidden Enrique.

And all YOU have to do is turn over that bigmouthed sombrero, said a naughty little voice somewhere in the back of my head.

Could I really sell him out like that, though? He trusted me. And I'd sort of made him a promise.

Don't do it, Jorge!

I could almost hear the big guy's voice in my head.

Don't even think about it! Dat's not nice!

Carter would be so disappointed in me for betraying someone's trust like that. So would Liza and Ernie.

And I'd probably deserve it, too.

"Uh, I will—I'll let you know if I see anything," I told the detective.

Gah! I'd just blown a once-in-a-lifetime shot at a state-of-the-art gaming setup. And all for some crummy old hat. Gosh, having a conscience really stinks sometimes...

CHAPTER 20

By the time 6:00 rolled around, the whole gang was gathered at Ernie's for a supposed sleepover, but in actuality, for Operation Museum Infiltrate Clue-Find Go-Go!

Yeah, definitely not the coolest-sounding mission name, but Carter had come up with it while we were brainstorming, and he was so proud of himself that nobody had the heart to change it. Operation Museum Infiltrate Clue-Find Go-Go! *did* pretty much sum up our plan, though. And that was to infiltrate the local civic center, find any clue the thieves may have accidentally left behind, and make it back to Ernie's without winding up in the cell across from Mr. Nez's.

"All right, we all know what's at stake, so let's

bring it in Three Musketeers style!" I said, putting out my fist. Two other fists joined mine, followed by a much bigger, much hairier one.

The owner of the hairier fist sounded sort of confused as he pointed out, "But there's one, two, three, cuatro of us."

"Don't sweat it," I told Carter. "there were four of them, too."

"Correction, there's *five* of us, amigos," said Enrique. "You think I'm just sitting up here to take the focus off of Jorge's abnormally large cranium?"

"Man, I should've traded you for that TV," I grumbled under my breath.

Anyway, since superhero costumes had worked for us the last time we'd gone sneaking around someplace uninvited, Ernie and I, being the superstitious baseball fans that we were, decided we better not risk jinxing it. So we went costume hunting in Ernie's garage.

You'd think cosplay would get old, but it just doesn't. The instant I put on my outfit, it felt like I'd jumped right back into the pages of my favorite comic book...

"Elevator up, please."

"But... why not use da window?"

"Can't believe they forget to close that! And especially after the robbery! Someone's totally getting fired..."

As we started in among the labyrinth of exhibits, the lousy old sombrero started flapping his brim again. "¡Oye, Sally! Long time no see! ¡Tomás! Looking chiseled (out of stone) as usual, buddy! Yo, Juan! How's the Paleolithic Age treating you?"

I glared up at him. "Keep it down! Who are you talking to anyway?!"

"Hey, I don't want to hear anything out of you, cabezón!" he snapped at me. "You've had real people to talk to all your life, but I spent the last thousand years having to make small talk with a bunch of glorified mannequins! So cut me some slack!"

Geesh . . . "All right, all right. Sorry I said anything."

Liza pointed her flashlight at a recently installed security camera in the corner near the ceiling and said, "Look! They must've recently installed security cameras!"

"*Should we hide?!*" hissed Ernie.

"A little too late for that," she told him. "But . . . it looks disconnected, doesn't it?"

It sort of did. There was a messy jumble of wires dangling out the back.

"Why would they do that?" Liza wondered aloud. "Finally install a security camera only to leave it disconnected?"

I shrugged. It didn't make any sense to me. Maybe they just never got around to plugging it in?

Suddenly off to my left came "¡Ándale, ándale! ¡Vaaaaaaamooos!"

I turned to see Carter all the way up on the white bony hump of a gigantic woolly mammoth skeleton, riding the eight thousand-year-old prehistoric beast with one arm flung back behind his head like some fur-covered rodeo cowboy.

"Carter, what are you doing??" I hissed.

"Dis da *biggest* caballo I ever seen!" he hissed back. "Can you imagine how much blood dis guy probably had?"

"Carter, that is *not* a horse! Now climb down from there before I count to five!" Oh my gosh, I was starting to sound like my grandma. *¡Órale!*

"Jorge, look at these fangs! They even bigger than mine!"

"Those are *tusks*, Carter," Ernie pointed out. "Now get down!"

"Everyone be quiet and spread out!" ordered Cat Burglar Girl. "Focus, people!"

Our flashlight beams bounced creepily off ancient Egyptian sarcophaguses and the hard, stern faces of Olmec stone heads as we wandered deeper into the maze of exhibits.

"This place looks so sad without me," said Enrique in a low voice. "Imagine me right in there, behind two inches of crystal-clear glass, glittering, drawing every single eye in the room."

"You're certainly drawing my eyes..." I muttered, glaring up at the big leather diva.

"You'd better control that animal, or we're all going to wind up in the back of a police car!" Enrique rasped down at me.

"Does he seem controllable to you?"

A moment later, Carter was bouncing excitedly up and down on the other side of the room by the archway that led into the adjoining hall. "Hey, I found a clue!"

"He's like the Energizer Bunny but with fangs," grumbled the sombrero. "Does he ever quit?"

"No," I said.

Then exactly two seconds later—

"I found another clue!" Carter whisper-shouted.

"See what I mean?" I said.

"Oh! And another!" Yep, Carter again.

"Uh, good going, Carter," I said, trying to sound positive. "Why don't you keep finding them and then I'll check them out once I'm done looking around over here."

"But, Jorge, I think these important!"

I sighed. Sometimes I wished I had that bloodsucker's energy. "Okay, Carter, show me..."

But they weren't just abandoned boots.

These boots happened to be connected to legs.

Six of them in total.

And those legs just so happened to be connected to bodies.

The bodies of the *burglars*!

I gulped, and on top of my head, Enrique gulped.

Carter, meanwhile, was busy checking out what

he believed were the sculptures to whom these boots belonged. Those furry chupacabra fingers were everywhere, pinching their cheeks, pressing their noses, gently rubbing their earlobes. It actually would've been pretty hilarious had my stomach not felt like it had crawled all the way up into the very tippy top of my throat.

"These *amazing*, Jorge! Dey feel so soft... so real!"

"Maybe that's because they *are* real, Carter," I pointed out. And it was right about then that I realized why the security camera was disconnected. These peeps had done the disconnecting!

Suddenly, something flashed in the dark. A knife. No, *a hook*! A shiny pirate's hook!

It came slashing sideways in a blurry arc, just barely missing Carter as he ducked and dodged it, and then barely missing me as I panicked and tripped backward over my own two feet.

"¡*CORRE!*" I screamed. Then, scrambling up, I turned and bolted back toward the main exhibit area, feeling absurdly like a cross between Antonio Banderas and Paul Revere (minus the horse, of course), shouting, "*THE THIEVES ARE COMING! THE THIEVES ARE COMING!*"

Liza and Ernie got the message pretty quick.

The moment they saw Carter and me come barreling from the other hall, our feet bicycling out behind us like on some old-school Saturday morning cartoon, they immediately turned tail and headed for the hills—or, more specifically, the window we'd climbed in through.

But with the gang of thieves on our butts—and gaining fast—that window looked like it was a million miles away!

Liza cast a desperate glance over her shoulder at the pursuing baddies and shouted, "We'll never make it!"

Then Enrique, hunkering down on my head, shouted: "Everybody split up!"

So we did. Liza and Carter went left, Ernie and I went right.

I raced past one exhibit after another—giant sea turtle fossils, rare moon rocks, flying kites from the Renaissance era—

And I nearly plowed right into a bony fur-covered chest as Carter came flying at me from the other direction!

Suddenly, the beady eyes of the super-buff burglar slid dangerously to me, and I did the only thing there was to do—I *ran*.

"No! No, no! Where are you going?" Enrique shouted down at me as I darted past a row of feathery Aztecan headdresses.

"What??" I shouted back.

"I know this place like the back of my hand! Just follow my lead!"

"Whatever!" So I followed Mr. Sombrero's lead.

Right at the T. rex!

Left at Leonardo da Vinci!

Left at Amelia Earhart!

And, surprise, surprise, I ran straight into another villain!

"I thought you said you knew this place like the back of your hand!" I roared at Enrique.

"Well, in all fairness, I don't really have hands, so..."

Great. A comedian!

"Oh my gosh! That was awesome!" I cheered. But what *wasn't* so awesome: not two seconds later, another villain melted out of the shadows of a Viking exhibit.

The tall, skinny one. Their slim fingers were closed tightly around the handle of a massive steel axe, and I heard myself gulp loudly enough to wake the mummies on the second floor.

"Uh, any tips for this one?" I squeaked.

"Yeah," said Enrique. *"RUN!"*

My feet didn't argue. They carried us through the zigzagging rows of exhibits as fast as they had ever carried me anywhere.

Unfortunately, it wasn't fast enough! The axe-wielding thief was right on my heels, the giant steel head of the axe poised to split me like an apple!

But before they could strike—

"Dude, ¡GRACIAS!" I shouted to the big guy.

The chupacabra was all fangy grins. "SupaCarter to da rescue!"

No sooner had he said that than the other two burglars appeared behind us. But that wasn't even the worst part. The worst part? These two were clutching *samurai swords*.

All of a sudden SupaCarter didn't look so super anymore. "SupaCarter no like swords."

"SupaJorge either," I admitted. "¡Vamos!"

Up ahead, Preteen Werewolf and Cat Burglar Girl were clawing desperately at the wall, trying to reach the window we'd climbed in through, but neither of their fingers could seem to latch on to the sill—it was too high! Thankfully, though, we had the big guy, and the moment we reached them, he started tossing us up and out the open window, one after another, before hopping up and climbing out himself.

Without wasting a second, the four of us darted wildly across the empty street in the moonlight and dove into a thick scrub of bushes that ran almost the length of the avenue.

"Liza, call 911!" I shouted breathlessly. But before her thumb could even hit the first 1, the trio of baddies jumped gracefully out the window and looked sneakily around for a moment before vanishing into the shadows up the street.

CHAPTER 21

"Let's just go to the cops!" I shouted when we were all back in Ernie's room later that night. "Let's go right now! Tell them everything!"

Liza looked at me like I was a couple of ice cream scoops short of a sundae. "You want us four kids, including the son of a prime suspect, to walk into the police station and admit to breaking and entering, trespassing, and the destruction of probably *millions* of dollars' worth of priceless antiques?"

"I was kind of hoping we could leave that last part out," I admitted sheepishly. "And maybe those other parts, too."

"Which part were you planning on leaving in? That we ran into some thieves who we can't identify because they were wearing masks, and we have no proof they were ever *actually* inside the civic center, but thanks to a talking sombrero, we know they were the same thieves from the robbery Ernie's dad is being accused of? I mean, if your goal is to give Mr. Nez some company in the slammer, that sounds like an excellent plan!"

Totally frustrated, I said, "Then what do we do, Liza?"

"Still working on that. But at least now we know those thieves are still in town and that they're still after the sombrero. Why else would they risk breaking into the museum again?"

Liza was right. As usual.

"Yeah, now we just have to put our Sherlock hats on," said Ernie.

"Sherlock didn't wear a hat," Enrique corrected him. "He wore a *deerstalker*. It's a cap. Completely different style of headwear. What do they even teach you kids in school nowadays?"

Ignoring him, I grumbled, "The mission was a bust. We didn't actually find any clues."

"Not so fast, amigo," interrupted Señor Sombrero. "I *did* find us a clue!"

"Of course I did!" he replied, like it was the most natural thing in the world. "I've always been pretty good at snatching things. It's really all about timing. See, I used your giant cabeza as bait, knowing that the thief would eventually find it irresistible to take a swipe at such a large and easy target, then once he missed, I snatched the hook right off his arm!"

"Take it easy with the giant head stuff, okay?" I warned.

"This is exactly what we needed!" Liza said excitedly as Enrique passed me Captain Hook's left hand.

I was shaking my head. "That crummy old thing? What could it possibly tell us?"

"Everything! Think about it, Jorge. The thief has probably had this forever! And we know that at the very least, he was touching it for however long they were in the museum tonight. That thing's probably *teeming* with his DNA!"

Teeming with DNA. *Yuck-o.* Pinching the hook like a dirty diaper, I held it away from me. "Someone else want to hold it?"

No takers.

"I bet just a thirty-second analysis of that hook will tell us everything, including what bodywash he uses!" said Liza.

"Not sure how his preference for soap is going to help us crack this case, but what kind of 'analysis' are you even talking about?"

"A forensic analysis. Any professional-grade forensic scanner will do the trick."

"Oh, of course!" I said. "A professional-grade forensic scanner. My grandma just bought me one for Christmas! It's in my room, still in the box. Let's go get it and we can finally crack this case!" I gave her my best *Gimme a break* look. "Seriously, Liza. How are we supposed to find one of those?"

"Well, the Boca Falls Police Department is bound to have at least one in their forensics lab."

"*The Boca Falls Police Department?* I thought you were the one who just said we couldn't go to the police?"

"We can't. We just need to borrow some of their equipment, that's all."

"You're kidding, right? Or are you seriously suggesting that we upgrade from breaking into museums to breaking into *police departments*? Because if that's your best idea, we might as well skip the middleman and lock ourselves up in jail while we're there."

"It's not as outlandish as you're making it sound, Jorge. All we really need is some cover."

Now Ernie was shaking his head. "Cover?"

"What we *need*," she said, that brilliant face of hers suddenly glowing with ideas, "is a middle school..."

"I thought you said we needed cover?" Carter looked confused. "Estoy confundido."

Liza slipped her phone out of her pocket. "I should be able to set this up for tomorrow."

"Set what up?" I asked as she started to dial. "Hey, who you callin'?"

"Mrs. Green."

"Mrs. Green? Why are you calling my social studies teacher?"

Liza's grin was a million watts bright and a million miles wide. "We need cover, remember?"

CHAPTER 22

"Now *that's* the kind of night that really gets your blood flowin'!" shouted Enrique when we were back in my room early the next morning, the sombrero doing a funny little waddle dance on my desk chair, sort of hopping around on his brim from side to side.

"You're not kidding. Only I was afraid it was going to start flowin' out of me," I admitted. "Did you see how close I was to being decapitated by Captain Hook back there?"

"That was a *close* shave! For both of us, amigo!" Enrique hopped up onto my desk, settling in comfortably between my stack of schoolbooks and my trusty catcher's mitt. "You did some beautiful work with your parry and counter. ¡Eso fue *fuego*! You've got a sweet left hook! And you," he said, turning to Carter, "you were an animal! The way you flying-kicked that one chasing us with an axe was a thing of beauty. It was like watching Picasso at work. That is, of course, if Picasso was a giant fur-covered ninja instead of a painter."

A proud, fangy grin split Carter's lips. "¡Gracias! But who's Picasso?"

We all burst out laughing again.

"You actually saved my life back there," I admitted, hardly believing that I was saying those words to a talking hat. And especially *this* talking hat. "You were amazing."

"Ah, it was nothing." With a wiggle of his brim, Enrique waved off the compliment. "Just returning the favor for helping me escape." He craned his crown around to face Carter. "Hey, those chips are pretty tasty. Toss me another."

As he caught one with his mouth, I said, "Man, you can really chow down, huh?"

"Like a grizzly bear!"

"But—where does it all *go*?"

"That, you *don't* wanna know." Then, hopping around on my desk, Enrique turned to look out my bedroom window, staring up at the still-visible slice of moon with as much longing as something without eyes or visible facial expressions can manage. "Oh, how I would love to have balled up a fist and socked one of those goons myself! Socked 'em right on the nose! Like you two did. I'm jealous."

When Carter let out a goofy giggle, Enrique said, "I'm not kidding. I really am jealous. I'd have happily given my chin strap to have gotten in on the action tonight. To have gotten a chance to do something. Even just run away."

The edges of his leathery brim had begun to sag with a kind of droopy sadness. It reminded me of the petals of a dying flower. It was honestly a little heartbreaking.

"Hey, man, forget about all that," I said, trying to cheer him up. "Like you told me—you're a sombrero. A head is your natural habitat or whatever. You were exactly where you were supposed to be."

Enrique fell silent for a few seconds. When he spoke again, his voice was low and rough. "I wasn't always the most beautiful sombrero there ever was."

Ninety-nine percent sure he was messing, I laughed, patting him on the point of his velvety crown. "Let me guess, you used to be a belt buckle?"

The hat didn't like that. "What? No! Who's ever heard of a talking belt buckle? How utterly ridiculous!" Swallowing a chill pill, he added, "No, I used to be just like you..."

"Just like *me*?" asked Carter with a little gasp of shock. "A chupacabra?"

"No! Not like you!" snapped Enrique. "Like *him*! I used to be a boy! A *human* boy!" He paused, clearing his... throat or whatever. "The people in my town used to call me El Sombrero because whenever I stole fruit or money I would always hide it in my old, beat-up ten-gallon sombrero. I was an orphan," he added sadly. "It was how I learned to survive."

I was getting ready to laugh again, only... he didn't sound like he was kidding. Not even a little. You could almost feel the sadness weighing down his words. "But I don't get it," I said. "If you really were a boy, how'd you end up as a... hat?"

"*Because of la bruja!*" Enrique erupted. "Haven't you ever heard any fairy tales? Those kinds of things *actually* happen in real life!" Then, flexing the wide circle of his brim the way a manta ray flexes its fishy wings, he seemed to settle down again. "But I don't blame you. Once upon a time, I didn't believe in fairy tales either."

"What happened with la bruja?" asked the chupacabra.

There were a few seconds of absolute silence, during which I couldn't help but wonder if Enrique had suddenly fallen asleep or something. But then he said, "I'm not going to lie: she and I used to be good friends. I'd see her go in and out of my village all the time. I used to sit by the gate begging every now and then, and she would always toss a coin in my ten-gallon sombrero when she passed by. *Siempre.* But then one day," he said, "I heard about the treasure she'd stolen—how she plundered those seven lavishly wealthy cities. And I said to myself, *There's no way I'm going to sit around here with one measly coin in my hat when this bruja has an entire hoard of treasure!* So I decided to steal it from her. Steal all of it! Or at least as much as I could fit in my trusty sombrero."

And just like that, the realization smacked into me like a line drive to the gut. "Oh my gosh!" I shouted. "You're the pickpocket kid from the El Dorado legend!"

"That is me," Enrique admitted, dragging the words out like he very much wished it wasn't.

No wonder he'd been able to snatch the hook away all slick-like! The guy was a pro! "Dude, how old are you?"

"It's never polite to ask a sombrero its age."

"Oh, sorry." Wait. Was he messing with me?

"Anyway," he continued, almost sadly now, "the next time la bruja passed the gate, I followed her all the way back to her secret mountain castle, where I knew she'd hidden the treasure. I made it pretty far in, too, all the way to the treasure room. But that's as far as I got before she caught me."

"So the treasure is real?" I whispered.

Enrique's voice dripped with old regrets. "The treasure is real."

Whoa. That had me sitting up pretty straight. "¡No inventes! And you know where it is?"

"WHAT DO I LOOK LIKE? A TALKING TREASURE MAP?" he suddenly exploded. "AND WHY DO YOU CARE? SO YOU CAN USE IT FOR YOUR OWN GREEDY, TWISTED, SELFISH PLEASURE?!"

¡Órale! This guy was SUPER touchy! "I was just wondering, man. Don't bust a stitch over it."

After a few moments, Enrique said, "Perdóname, I get a little worked up about that treasure. Lots of history between us... lots and lots of history."

CHAPTER 23

It had taken Liza less than twenty-four hours to execute her master plan, and by 10:00 a.m. the following morning, almost half the kids in our grade were lined up in three neat single-file lines out in front of the local police station, waiting for our private tour.

Ernie and I were still in shock that Liza had been able to pull it off. I mean, you'd think that arranging a short-notice field trip like this would be impossible. But I guess when you're every teacher's favorite student, the impossible is possible.

Lieutenant Avery was our tour guide, and after introducing herself and showing off her shiny badge, she led us around to the back of the station where the kennels were located, so we could meet the police pooches. We even got to feed a few treats to Sergeant Scruff, a semiretired German Shepherd whose main job was to help train some of the new pups.

After that, we headed inside to check out the booking room on the first floor and the sketch artist's office on the second floor, where Officer Dominguez, the resident Picasso, drew a family portrait of our teachers.

Anyway, it was on floor número tres that things got really interesting. Just as we were strolling down the long hallway on our way to tour the dispatch center, Liza yanked Ernie and me out of line.

"This way!" she hissed, pulling us into a pitch-dark room right next to the janitor's closet.

"Where are we?!" Ernie whispered. But he really didn't need to. Because the instant our eyes adjusted to the dimness, the answer was pretty obvious.

The third-floor forensics lab looked straight off the set of a Hollywood detective movie. The only difference? All the fancy-looking lab equipment in here actually did stuff.

Everywhere I looked, there were microscopes and blinking lights and scientific instruments.

But it was the high-tech monstrosity beeping and humming in the middle of the cold, dry room that captured my attention.

Standing almost five feet tall—and looking like a space-age cross between a scanner, a high-powered microwave, and Bobby Flay's fanciest ice cream maker—was the forensics scanner. Or at least that's what the tag on the side claimed.

Without wasting a moment, Liza unzipped her backpack, grabbed Captain Hook's golden hand, and laid it carefully on the smooth see-through surface of the scanner thingamajig. Then she slid into a chair in front of a nearby monitor, began tapping away at the square-shaped keys, and suddenly the scanner roared awake behind us, nearly making Ernie and me color our undies!

A pane of flickering red light shot straight up out of the machine's crystal surface, and I half expected to see Vision being created, cell by cell, in some nearby incubator.

"Gosh, that thing is loud!" Ernie whispered.

"Looks like we got something." Liza's grinning face glowed pale blue in the light of the monitor. "*All sorts* of somethings, as a matter of fact!"

Peeking over her shoulder, squinting in the dark, I whispered, "What does it say?"

"No time." Liza plugged a mini hard drive into the

side of the computer tower, dragged a mess of files into it, then quickly exited the program and clicked off the screen. "I'll look through it later. But right now, it's time to make like a rock, and roll!"

But no sooner had we all spun around to go than the door burst open!

CHAPTER 24

I barely had time to feel the first tickles of fear when in walked—

A CHUPACABRA?!

"CARTER?" Ernie screeched in disbelief.

The grinning bloodsucker quietly shut the door, giggling to himself as he did.

"Carter, what are you doing here?!" Liza whisper-shouted. "Someone could have seen you!"

"Don't worry! They did!" said Enrique from on top of Carter's head. "And they just waved and smiled!"

My panic quickly morphed to outrage. "WHAT?!"

"Check out my badge!" Carter said proudly, tapping what really did look like some kind of official police badge pinned to his doggy collar.

"Where did you get that?!" I shrieked.

"From Scruff," Enrique happily informed us. "Down in the kennels. He's a real cool pooch."

"We traded him a half-eaten roast beef sandwich from Arby's," explained Carter.

Liza gaped. "You bribed a *police officer*?!"

I gasped. "You guys went to Arby's?!"

"Easy there," said Enrique. "We had to grab a bite somewhere. Even sombreros need to eat."

"The curly fries were *fuego*!" shouted Carter with a dreamy look in his eyes.

"But how'd you even find us?" Ernie screeched, practically hyperventilating by this point. And who could really blame the kid? I was right there with him!

"Chups tracked your scent," said Enrique. "He's got quite the talented nose! Well, *that* or you three really need baths..."

"Chups? Who the heck is *Chups*?" I snapped. "Are you two giving each other pet names now?"

Carter grinned. "Uh-huh! He's Hatty!"

I had this sudden awful sensation of being trapped in some spicy-burrito-induced nightmare. I had to wake up.

I *had* to get out of here!

As if reading my mind, Ernie hissed, "We have to get out of here already! This is an emergency, people!"

Still feeling like I was dreaming, I started to hear a loud, shrill ringing that sounded suspiciously like a fire alarm. Then I looked around and saw why.

Carter had pulled the fire alarm by the door!

"*CARTER! WHY'D YOU DO THAT?*" Liza exploded.

"It say 'Pull in case of emergency,'" he replied with an embarrassed look. "And Ernie jess said it's an emergency, no?"

"And if there was a sign there that said 'Smack yourself in case of emergency,' would you have done that too?"

Carter shrugged. "Yeah?"

An instant later, I heard more trouble—the terrifying pounding of running feet! Someone out in the hall yelled, "I think it came from this floor! We'll grab the fire extinguishers and check forensics! You clear the building!"

¡Dios mío! They're coming straight for us!

"EVERYONE HIDE!" I shrieked.

"I'm going to scream!" hissed Enrique. Liza glared daggers at him and mashed an index finger against her lips.

An instant later, we heard the click of the door being closed. After a minute, Ernie rushed over to try the handle. "It won't open!" he hissed. "He must've locked it from the outside!"

"What's gonna happen to us??" Carter asked, his voice trembling.

"Eventually they'll find us, and then we're *dead*!" screeched Ernie.

"But I am too beautiful to die!" cried el sombrero.

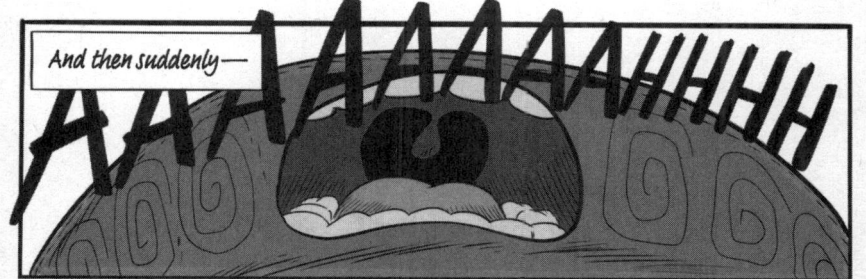

CHAPTER 25

After an ordeal like that, you'd think that at least one of us would've had some sort of shock-related trauma. But we were mostly okay. Liza had gone straight home after school to start sorting through all the info the fancy-schmancy forensics machine had pulled off the pirate hook. We'd asked if we could help, but she said we would only get in the way (which was probably true), so Ernie, Enrique, Carter, and I went back to my house, where we'd spent the last couple of hours playing the four-player campaign version of the new Lord of the Rings video game Ernie had left at my house a couple weeks ago.

"I can't believe we actually pulled that off!" said E-dog as he waited for his Legolas avatar to re-spawn after getting thrown off the top of the Lonely Mountain by the Pale Orc. "Talk about pulling a rabbit out of our hats!"

Enrique grinned at that. "Good one! That's actually my favorite magic trick!"

"Pulling a goat out of a hat would be more magical, I think," said Carter thoughtfully.

"Sure!" agreed Enrique. "But much more painful for the hat."

"I thought we were *toast*," I admitted, serving up some slabs of orc roast with the gleaming edge of the Goblin-cleaver.

"Imagine if we actually cracked this case!" said the sombrero, the cord of his chin strap twitching excitedly. "Just picture the headline! 'Genius talking sombrero and his team of misfits solve the most important museum heist of all time!'"

"But I not a misfit," said Carter seriously. "I can fit pretty much anywhere. Chupacabras *extremely* flexible."

"And I'm pretty sure this isn't the most important museum heist *of all time*," I couldn't help pointing out.

"I'm involved, no?" The hat gave me one of his

usual smug looks. "So that automatically makes it the most important."

"Not going to argue with you," I said, grinning like a dog with a bone. "I'm just happy we made it out of that place without having been read our rights. I seriously can't remember the last time I felt *this* relieved! Actually, that's a lie. I felt about this relieved when we first came face-to-face with the thieves in the museum."

Carter looked confusedamundo. "I don't get it."

"Yeah, how did almost getting *decapitated* make you feel relieved?" asked Ernie with a sideways smirk.

"Because that was our first hard proof that your dad was actually innocent, bro! Up to then, that man put the capital *G* in guilty. And probably all the rest of the letters, too!"

Ernie's smile instantly turned upside down. "Hold up. You thought my dad was *guilty*?"

"Ha! Just a little," I said with a snort.

"But I told you he didn't do it, Jorge. And you said you believed me."

"Yeah, I know that's what I *said*, but..."

"But *what*?" demanded Ernie.

"But that's just something people say, isn't it? To support each other. I mean, I wanted you to feel like I had your back."

"When in reality you didn't?" With a shake of his head, Ernie tossed his controller onto my bed. "I think I'm done playing."

"Ernie, c'mon. Don't be like that!"

"No, Jorge! I *am* gonna be like that! How could you not believe me??"

"Because your dad looked super guilty, that's how! They even had him on video!"

"If someone would've accused your grandmother of committing some horrible crime and you told me she was innocent, I would've believed you!"

"Ernie, if someone accused my grandmother of committing a horrible crime, I would back them up—because it would probably be the truth!"

"Friends are supposed to trust each other, Jorge! Commander William T. Riker even said, 'Without trust, there's no friendship.' And you didn't trust me!"

¡Órale! This guy had a Star Trek quote for literally every situation. "Ernie, it's not like that."

"You mean it's not like my best friend secretly

didn't believe me, thought my dad was some low-down dirty crook the entire time, and then lied to my face about it?"

"Okay, it is like that," I had to admit. "But it sounds so much worse when you say it all accusingly like that."

E-dog pushed angrily to his feet. "I'm outta here."

"Ernie, whose idea was it to try to prove that your dad was innocent, huh? That was all me!"

"Yeah, except you didn't even believe it yourself!"

"So?"

"So?! That's my whole point! You didn't trust me!"

"Ernie—*chill*."

"You chill! I'm going home!"

CHAPTER 26

"They made this game too HARD!" I shouted a few minutes later, spiking my controller on my bed as my Bilbo avatar once again received the ole Burger King Whopper treatment, courtesy of an ill-tempered dragon. "This is so frustrating!"

No joke—I'd never felt so twisted up inside over a video game in my life. Like, *ever*!

"I don't think your frustrations have anything to do with this game, amigo," said Señor Know-It-All.

I wanted to glare at him. I really did. But for whatever reason, I just didn't feel like looking anyone in the eye at the moment—even if he didn't have any.

"What are you yapping about? We have this stupid thing on easy and we're getting flame-roasted faster and faster every time we rush the treasure room!"

Then the bigmouth hat came right out and said it. "Hey, are you going to be Mr. Cranky Pants all night or call your friend and apologize already? Because I don't know about you, but I don't see any way we'll be able to slay that overgrown lizard with this abysmally low level of morale!"

"You're saying *I* should apologize to Ernie? He's the one making macaroni out of a molehill! Or however that silly saying goes."

"You hurt your friend's feelings, which means *you're* the one who's got to apologize," said the sombrero like it had been inscribed in the Ten Commandments of Friendship or something.

"What do you know about feelings?" I grumbled. "You're just a fancy piece of goat hide..."

But unfortunately, it wasn't just him. My favorite bloodsucking furball was also apparently on Team Ernie. "He's right, Jorge. You hurt Ernie. You need to tell him you sorry."

"But I'm in the right here, Carter! I didn't do anything. Ernie's the one blowing this whole thing out of proportion! Why should I have to apologize?"

And that's when Bigfoot's long-lost goat-slurping cousin looked straight at me with those round, wise eyes of his and said something that I will never forget.

"Jorge, there's an old chupacabra proverb dat go, 'It's not important to always be right, but it's important to always be *kind*.'"

CHAPTER 27

I don't know how or why those words hit me so hard, but they did. I even got this big lump in my throat! I guess it was the fact that deep down inside, I knew there was a lot of truth in them.

Still, it was weird to be taking life lessons from a guy whose idea of a Happy Meal usually included a very *un*happy farm animal. I decided I needed a fresh perspective on all this. Well, a *human* perspective, anyway. So I called Liza.

She was in the middle of looking through the scanner readings, but said she had a few minutes to talk. I hadn't even gotten into what went down between Ernie and me, but it was like she already knew. "Jorge, what'd you do?"

"*Me*? Why are you blaming me?"

"You didn't start whatever happened?"

"No, you're right. I did. But I don't like that you just *assumed* it was me. And how did you know something even happened?"

"Because it's prime gaming time and you're holding a phone and not your controller."

Huh. A fair point.

Anyway, I told her the whole story and surprise, surprise, she was also on Team Ernie.

"Honestly? I feel kind of terrible about it, too," I admitted.

"Well, then tell that to Ernie. Tell him how you feel."

"But that's not the Lopez way! We never talk about our feelings! We keep them locked away deep down until they eat us up from the inside! It helps remind us how tough we are."

"Jorge, just tell him you didn't mean to hurt his feelings. Say you're sorry."

"But I already tried, Liza! He wouldn't listen. I don't think I've ever seen Ernie this upset."

"So maybe more action, less words, then?"

I blinked. "What exactly are you suggesting?"

"You know what."

Unfortunately, I did. "Liza, I am *not* dressing up like a Starfleet geek!"

See, a few weeks ago, Ernie, being the biggest Trekkie that has ever walked the face of this planet, had bought us both "authentic" *Star Trek* costumes off this website that auctions old movie and TV memorabilia. He said he thought it would be a total "mind meld" if the two of us dressed up like real-life USS *Enterprise* crew members while riding our bikes around the neighborhood, but the whole thing was just sooo ridiculously uncool that I couldn't bring myself to do it. And I wasn't about to start now.

"Listen, I've got my hands full here," said Liza, "but you know what you have to do, capitán."

"*No!* That ain't happening! I am *not* dressing up as Mexican Captain Kirk!"

I could hear the laughter in her voice as she said, "Bye, Jorge."

"I won't do it, Liza! Are you listening to me? My resistance is NOT futile!"

The following day...

CHAPTER 28

Yeah, I wasn't a happy camper as the three of us made our way to Liza's early the next morning.

The good news? Ernie was already there when we arrived, climbing up the porch steps in the hot sunshine.

The even better news? The instant he saw me—or more specifically, saw me wearing that ridiculous USS captain's uniform—his entire face suddenly lit up like the Rockefeller Center Christmas tree and he ran over, throwing his arms around me in a giant abrazo.

Then he started apologizing, telling me how sorry he was about yesterday and how silly he felt for having walked out on us and all that.

Talk about a total emotional fliparoo. But I guess sometimes actions do speak louder than words, huh?

Anyway, I told him to forget it, that it was really my fault, after all. That I should've trusted him from the beginning—and just like that, we were best buds again!

"C'mon, dude, do it!" Ernie begged.

I shook my head firmly. "That I won't do."

"Oh, c'mon! You're already all dressed up!"

"Ernie, there are some things a self-respecting Chicano just *can't* do..."

"C'mon, Jorge! *One time!*"

I squeezed my eyes shut. Oh, the humiliating things we do for friends...

Then, with a loud sigh, I raised my hand in that

überfamous Star Trek V-shaped salute, and with another loud sigh I repeated that übergeeky line: "Live long and prosper."

Ernie, of course, was over the moon.

"There it is!" he cheered, returning the salute.

I glanced carefully around to make sure there were no eyewitnesses to what I was about to do. Then I said, in my best Mr. Spock impersonation, "I think getting mad at each other was *highly* illogical."

"Wait till you guys hear what I found!" Liza said excitedly as the five of us huddled around the large writing desk in the middle of her room a few minutes later. "You're going to flip your lids!"

Enrique didn't like that one. "Was that a hat joke?"

Liza grinned. "Little bit. Now check this out!" she said, shaking the mouse to wake up her computer monitor. "Here's a readout of all the material the forensic scanner was able to detect on the pirate's hook. The substances are listed by weight and in descending order; and as you can clearly see, right at the top of the list is *Mycetophyllia danaana*! How cool is that?"

"Uh, in English this time, please?" I said.

"Calcified remnants of the ridged cactus, to be specific," she not-so-helpfully explained.

"OK, maybe try in Spanish now, because I'm still not getting it."

"It's a rare species of coral reef, Jorge. It's only found in the Caribbean. Which, of course, makes perfect sense, considering the hook's last owner."

I gaped. "You know who last owned it?"

"Yep! Thanks to the maker's mark right here." She double-clicked a file on her desktop and what looked like a zoomed-in high-def photo of the hook popped up on the screen. "It's pretty tiny as far as these kinds of markings go, but it was enough to help me track down the owner."

"Enough with the drumroll, Liza! Who owns that thing?"

"A Señor Víctor Vásquez. *Pirate* Víctor Vásquez, to be specific."

"Hold up—are you saying the dude I went mano a mano with at the museum was a real-life pirata?!"

Ernie's face was a mask of shock. "Pirates are after the treasure of El Dorado??"

"They may be," said Liza, "though in Víctor's

case, I suspect he'd have to be one pretty determined scallywag, because his ship sank somewhere north of the Greater Antilles after tangoing with a hurricane in the year 1834. Víctor and his crew were never seen or heard from again."

"SO THEY'RE UNDEAD PIRATE *GHOSTS*?!" Ernie screeched. Now, that might've sounded totally ridiculous to the average person, but after some of the stuff we'd seen in this town (present talking-hat company included), you'd be silly to rule *anything* out.

Liza sighed. "Not at all where I was going, Ernie, but A-plus for creativity. Remember, ghosts could walk right into a museum. *Through* the walls. They wouldn't need to pick the lock on the skylight."

True! And it was a total relief, too. Because I didn't think I could deal with another supernatural entity so soon after our haunted piñata friend. I took a second to let my pulse return to normal before saying, "So what's going on, Liza?"

"I'm getting to it." Sliding aside Captain Hook's hand, she pointed to a stack of papers splattered with bright yellow and orange highlights. "Now listen to this. The forensic scanner also found trace amounts of hydrocarbons."

"Inglés, por favor," said Enrique.

"It's another word for petroleum, also known as crude oil. That's what those giant deep-sea drilling rigs suck out of the earth's crust."

"Is dat like the earth's... *blood*?" Carter asked, his furry lips smacking hungrily together.

"You could say that. Anyway, this is where I started putting two and two together," said Liza. "See, a couple of years back I did a science fair project, trying to find a way to clean up the world's oceans. My idea was to develop an ultra-absorbent sponge-like material that could be used to help contain the damage from oil spills and leaks. I couldn't exactly get it to work. But the point is, I remember coming across a news article about this huge oil spill in the Caribbean near Exuma, Bahamas. So I looked into it, and it matches perfectly with what we know about the pirate Víctor Vásquez! Remember, his ship had sunk not too far from there. So now feast your eyes on this—"

With the flourish of a Las Vegas magician, she whipped out what looked like a scan of some old Bahamian newspaper article.

The headline read:

**TREASURE TROVE DISCOVERED
FIVE MILES OFF THE COAST OF EXUMA**

"I found that in an archive online," she said. "In 2008, a team of treasure hunters discovered what they believe to be a pirate shipwreck!"

"I don't get it," said Carter with a fangy frown.

Then Liza turned the paper over to show the rest of the article. It came with a large black-and-white photo of the treasure-finding divers.

There were three of them—two short bodybuilder types, with biceps the size of watermelons, and a very tall, very skinny lady.

The three amigos were standing on the sandy shore of a gorgeous Bahamian beach with a treasure chest half-sunk in the powdery sand between them, holding up pearly necklaces, handfuls of pirate loot, and—

A hook.

No, *the* hook!

OUR hook!

At that moment all the puzzle pieces came slamming together in my brain, and I was amazed that my eyes didn't go blasting out of their sockets and through Liza's bedroom window!

"Lookie, lookie, I found hookie!" Liza—or should I say, Vegan Sherlock over here—was grinning from one SAVE THE POLAR BEARS earring to the other.

"THAT'S THE HOOK!" I shouted, hardly believing my eyes.

"And those are definitely the museum-robbing rascals!" growled Enrique, jabbing angrily at the paper with the leathery edge of his brim. Had it been an index finger, he would've busted a hole through all three of their faces. But he was right!

"It's them, all right!" Liza agreed. "The article goes on to talk about their haul—somewhere in the neighborhood of one hundred thousand dollars. Pretty good for a weekend dive in the Caribbean. And it also mentions the pirate hook, calling it the crown jewel of the discovery."

"But is there a better picture of them?" I asked her, pawing through a few of the papers spread out on her desk. "We can't exactly see their faces. How are we supposed to give their description to the police?"

"Unfortunately, this is the only picture I could find. And believe me, I looked. But I did find a little more info. This is from a small newspaper in the Cayman Islands. Listen to this"—Liza brought out another scan and began to read—"'Polish business partners and ex–circus performers discover a long-lost pirate ship and score a boatload of loot in the process.'"

"Aha! They're ex–circus performers!" shouted Ernie. "That narrows things down a bit."

"Sure, now we just have to call up the Ringling Brothers and ask them if any of their ex-employees happen to be rotten treasure-hunting thieves," said Enrique.

A sombrero with jokes. I'd seen it all now.

"Wait!" I shouted suddenly. "¡Mira! The article gives a name!" It was right there in the second paragraph. The woman was Zofia Wiśniewski. "White Pages.com! Go, go, go!"

"Already went," Liza said. "The name's not showing up anywhere. I was only able to link it to a PO box in Eastern Europe that was rented almost a decade ago."

"So that's it?" It seemed like all our leads went nowhere.

"I'm not finished," she continued. "Check this out." She clicked another link and the stark black-and-white lettering of a third newspaper scan popped up on the screen. This one was an interview with the lady, where she talked a bit about their past, and how they'd gotten into treasure hunting.

According to Zofia, the whole treasure-hunting idea came from a pact they'd made with each other a few years before. Supposedly, the circus her family had started (and that all three of them grew up in) had been taken over by creditors about a decade ago when the business fell on some hard times. Having her family's legacy taken away apparently devasted Zofia, and she swore she'd find a way to get her hands on enough money to start a new circus—"The grandest and most extravagant circus ever!" Her words. And I guess treasure hunting was that way.

"I can't believe it!" I said, cracking up. "We're up against a bunch of circus clowns! Legit payasos!"

"Clowns who think they're pirates!" added Ernie, sending Carter into stitches.

Liza, on the other hand, hadn't joined the giggle party. "Guys, don't underestimate these people," she warned us. "They got some heavy stats. It says right there that Zofia is a fourth-generation aerialist specializing in the trapeze and aerial silks, and that she's a trained marksman. The twins are professional acrobats and powerlifters, as well as champion swordsmen. These people are world-class athletes at the peak of their prowess. Call them all the names you want, but they seem both extremely talented and extremely motivated to me."

I shook my head, staring dazedly down at the

newspaper photo again. "So, world-class circus performers turned treasure hunters, an old pirate's hook, a talking sombrero. This has got to be the weirdest spot we've found ourselves in yet! So, what's the plan, Liza? How are we going to find these twerps? Let's put our thinking caps on!"

"Why waste your time with some silly cap when you have a handsome goatskin sombrero right here?" asked Enrique annoyedly.

I sighed. "It's just an expression."

"Don't worry. I already know what to do," said Vegan Sherlock with a look that I knew meant business. "It's time to put our dialers to work."

"Dialers?"

"Dialing fingers."

"Who are we calling?"

"Every motel, hotel, and inn inside the Boca Falls city limits. We're going hunting ... for treasure hunters!"

CHAPTER 29

The next three days were the busiest seventy-two hours of my entire life. First, there were close to one *hundred* hotels and motels in the greater Boca Falls area. And that wasn't even counting all the smaller bed-and-breakfast joints or short-term rentals where someone could sneakily shack up for a week or two without even having to show a driver's license.

As if that wasn't bad enough, we had the dark shadow of Ernie's dad's court case looming over our heads like a proverbial guillotine. The trial was set to begin next month and the board of directors of the museum was seeking a maximum sentence.

Ira Baddensworth was obviously fuming, too. He was showing up on all the local TV stations, berating our town. "First a robbery and now vandalism! This has to be the most sinister town in the entire union!"

Meanwhile, the two trench coat detectives were turning up their investigation. I started seeing them everywhere, questioning people anyplace you could think of—the grocery store, the local library, the movie theater, even the hair salon! They paid Liza a personal visit, too.

And just when you thought things couldn't get any worse, things *did*. On the first Sunday of the month, the police found one of the stolen museum items—la bruja's riddle. And where do you think they found it? In the trunk of Ernie's dad's silver Cadillac, of course.

The discovery had not-so-surprisingly devastated Ernie's mom. Ernie even had to miss two whole days of school to take care of her. It was terrible. It hit the rest of us pretty hard, too, but since we knew Mr. Nez was innocent, it only strengthened our determination to prove it.

And now it became obvious that the whole thing was a setup! Somebody out there was playing the world's highest stakes game of Pin the Tail on the Donkey... only the "tail" was a daring museum robbery and the "donkey" happened to be *Ernie's dad*.

We knew exactly who it was, too. The three treasure-hunting weasels. The only problem was we didn't know who the heck they were underneath those masks, and we couldn't seem to sniff out their current hideout.

Things were getting serious, and looking seriously *bad*.

Hopefully Liza had another plan up those 100 percent non-animal, hemp sleeves of hers, because I wasn't feeling too good about our current one.

CHAPTER 30

That night, a deep and peaceful silence jerked me out of sleep. Now, I know what you're thinking: *Jorge, what are you talking about? Loud noises jerk people out of sleep, not silences.*

And normally, I'd agree. But during the past few days of sleeping in the same room with Señor Screams in His Sleep and a three-hundred-pound cryptid who snores like a water buffalo with some serious nasal congestion, nighttime silence had been pretty hard to come by. I'd gotten used to the midnight concerts, so suddenly having golden peaceful silence felt totally wrong.

I sat up drowsily to see what was wrong with Carter and Enrique—pretty sure that *something* had to be—and that's when I realized that they weren't sleeping at all. In fact, they weren't even there!

I jumped out from under my covers in a wild panic. Had they somehow been lured out of the room by the treasure hunters? Had they been captured, kidnapped—maybe *worse*?

Or maybe Carter had finally given into his instincts and eaten Enrique!

I had just picked up my phone to dial 911 (well, more like Liza-1-1) when a scraping sound had my head snapping around to see the long, scraggly form of Carter quickly climbing in through my bedroom window with Enrique riding proudly on his furry head.

"¡Oye! ¡Oye! We got big news!" called el sombrero.

"Where have you two been?" I snapped.

"Dat's the news!" said Carter, panting a little. "We found dem, Jorge! We found dem!"

"No, no, no. Let's start from the beginning!" Enrique interrupted, pumping his pointy crown like a fist.

"Start wherever you want, but one of you better start talking!" I whisper-shouted.

"Okay, here goes! The big fella and I got bored earlier, so we went out."

"Hit the pause button right there—you 'went out'?!"

"Are you going to let me talk or just ask silly questions? Because both can't happen at the same time."

I bit my tongue. El sombrero continued. "Anyway, the big guy and I decided to spend a night out on the town. We thought it would be fun to hit a disco club, mingle with—"

"You went *disco dancing*?" Yeah, that was where I drew the line. Chupacabras and talking hats hitting a disco club.

"It was his idea!" Carter pointed an accusing furry finger up at Enrique.

"Tattletale!" the hat hissed down at him.

"QUIET!" I snapped. "What were you two doing at a dance club??"

"Dancing, what else? And you should've seen me under that giant disco ball!" he yapped on. "My crown glittering, my brim glistening! Oh, and our dance moves! They were straight *candela*!"

"What dance moves?!" I roared. "You don't even have a body!"

"Hey, don't get nasty with me!" Señor Sombrero warned. "You don't need a body when you can shake your brim like this!" He demonstrated, and it was as if Shakira had been transformed into a wide-brimmed hat! I'm not kidding. The guy could pop and lock like it was nobody's business!

Carter said, "And check this out!" Then the big guy busted out a series of hip shakes, lock steps, and body rolls that would've made the cast of *Dancing with the Stars* jealous.

I was almost speechless. "But how did you two even get into the club?"

"It was costume night," explained Enrique. "Everybody was dressed up. We went as Ranchero Chewbacca!"

"That was my idea!" Carter said with a fangy grin.

"Anyway, they were having their annual dance-off. A pretty prestigious competition, I should mention. So naturally, we *had* to enter."

"Of course you did." Because why *wouldn't* a talking sombrero and a seven-foot-tall blood-guzzling monster enter a dancing competition? "Okay, and . . . ?"

"And we kind of . . . *won*." Grinning like a hyena, Carter brought a huge gold trophy from behind his furry back.

I almost lol'd. Seriously. If this whole thing hadn't been so completely reckless of them, I would have probably been rolling around on the floor right about now.

"That better not be the big news," I warned them.

"You've got to admit, it's pretty big news. But no," said the dancing hat. "Here's where our little story gets weird."

"Weirder than a chupacabra and a bigmouthed sombrero disco dancing?" Call me skeptical, but I couldn't see it.

"Tell him about the team that got second place," Enrique said.

"No! I don't want to hear any more about that silly dance-off! I only want to hear about the supposed big news!"

"*Dey* are the big news!" shouted Carter.

"What are you talking about?" I snapped.

"About two very short, very buff tipos painted head to toe in green," said Enrique.

"Huh?"

"That was dey costume!" Carter explained.

I shook my head. "You mean, like the Incredible Hulk?"

"Yes, the Edible Hulk! Dat one!" I opened my mouth to tell him that it was "incredible," not "ed-

CHUPACARTER AND THE SCREAMING SOMBRERO

ible," but since Carter pretty much saw everything (and everybody) as a potential snack, I decided not to bother. "Dey had some wow moves!"

"Acrobat-style moves!" added Enrique. "We just barely edged them out on the judge's scorecards!"

Fed up already, I whisper-shouted, "Guys, I told you I don't want to hear anything else about that ridiculous dance—"

And that's when it hit me. "Wait. Did you say two super-short, super-buff guys?"

Carter was all fangs and gums. "Uh-huh!"

"With acrobat moves?"

"*Circus* acrobat moves," added Señor Dance-a-Lot.

"It was dem, Jorge! One even had the small circus tent tattoo on his forearm jess like in da newspaper!"

My voice was thick with disbelief. "So what'd you two do?"

"We followed them, of course!" said Enrique. "¿Qué te crees? You think you're the only one with a brain inside that giant head of yours?!"

"All right, all right. Take it easy with the cabeza jokes. What happened next?"

We followed those musclebound treasure hunters down alleys, across deserted intersections, through a steamy tropical jungle—

"A steamy jungle? ¿Neta?" I didn't even know New Mexico had tropical jungles.

"No, not really," admitted the sombrero. "I only threw that in there to add a little more drama."

"Then what happened?"

"Then we lost them!"

"You *WHAT*? How?"

An embarrassed frown tugged on the chupacabra's lips. "I spotted an ardillita..."

"Carter, you went chasing a squirrel and blew our best and *only* hope of finding these thieves?!"

"Hey, don't get all bent out of shape, cabezón! We found them again."

My eyes bugged in shock and relief. "You did?"

"Of course! But then I got distracted by this luxury hat shop up the street. They were having a special on leather oils. I *love* me some nice leather oils..." At my laser-eyed death glare, the sombrero held up the edges of his brim like hands. "Cálmate, cálmate, calm down. We found them again right after that."

¡Híjole! This story had more twists than a telenovela!

"Yeah, I spotted dem," said Carter.

"Well, you *sniffed* them," corrected Enrique.

"Ah, sí. I sniffed dem."

"You sniffed them and I spotted them. Beauty and the Beast—a perfect tag team!"

"Okay, slow down," I said. "Let's not start with the high fives and back patting just yet. Where'd you follow them to?"

"Château Blanche, a nice little French hotel a few blocks north of the disco club."

Now it was time for high fives and back patting! I threw my arms around my fur-covered best bud. "You guys did it! We've gotta tell Ernie and Liza!"

CHAPTER 31

As you can imagine, Liza's and Ernie's cabezas nearly exploded early the next morning when I served the tea about Carter and Enrique's big night at the disco club.

It was the break we'd all been waiting for! But the situation was still super tricky. After a team brainstorm, we realized we couldn't go spill the frijoles to the authorities just yet.

First off, even if they believed our story—which they wouldn't—a detective wouldn't legally be able to search the thieves' hotel room without a warrant. And they wouldn't be able to get a warrant without some pretty solid evidence.

Worse, if a police officer *did* happen to believe us and they started asking those circus clowns some unpleasant questions, the villains were likely to get jumpy and skip town, leaving Ernie's dad all alone to take the rap for the museum heist.

No, we'd have to handle this ourselves. At least, we would have to handle the evidence-finding part ourselves. Good thing for us, Liza had already come up with the perfect plan!

All we had to do was scope the place out, wait for the musclebound acrobats to step out for something (maybe another disco competition), then sneak into their room and find proof that they'd orchestrated the robbery. The ancient Aztecan dagger was still missing, so finding that tucked away in their things would just about clinch it.

The only thing we had to watch out for was that there were three of these clowns, not just the two mini-Hulks. But as long as we waited for the "muscle" of the crew to clear out, even if the "brains" was still hanging out inside the hotel room, we should be able to deal with her. Well, Carter could, anyway.

Fortunately for us, Hotel Château Blanche wasn't too far, only about a twenty-minute bike ride from Ernie's. Also, fortunately for us, today was a Saturday, which meant that Operation Pardon My French was a go!

CHAPTER 32

Our battle plan was as follows:

>PHASE ONE: Enter the hotel undetected.

>PHASE TWO: Locate the employee changing room.

>PHASE THREE: Change into housekeeper uniforms and find a universal passkey.

>PHASE FOUR: Use Carter's nose to track the villains' room.

Those were the four key phases of the operation and we were running through them like a well-oiled machine!

The moment the elevator doors slid open on the fifth floor, Carter picked up the acrobats' scent.

"They can run, but they can't hide!" said Señor Sombrero, quoting my favorite Tom Cruise movie.

Only I should have known it wasn't going to be that easy...

Behind door number one, we found a family of five feasting on a platter of Korean barbecue.

Behind door number two, two old ladies were watching TV and gobbling pulled pork sandwiches.

Behind door number three was a full-blown pizza party.

"We're so sorry!" Liza announced for the third time in the last two minutes. "We'll be back later to clean up!"

Out in the hall, I hissed, "Carter, what are you doing?"

The chupacabra looked about as embarrassed as a skunk in a perfume shop. "It's my stomach, Jorge! It's tricking my nose! I sooo hungry!"

"We should never have tried this before lunch," sighed Enrique.

I grabbed the vampire Sasquatch by the humps of his bony, fur-covered shoulders and pulled us almost eye to eye.

"Carter, head in the game!" I said, channeling my inner coach. "This is serious! We don't know how long those two are going to be out!"

"This has to happen now!" rasped Liza.

I saw the big guy's pooch-like nostrils flare. Saw the long-lashed lids of his mismatched eyes—first the blue one, then the green—narrow with fierce concentration.

I knew that look. It was Carter's game face. He was ready to rock and roll.

"Okay," he whispered intensely. "I focus! I find dey room right now!"

His talented schnoz led us halfway down the hall to room number 502, where a DO NOT DISTURB sign dangled from the door handle.

Parking our trolley by the door, Liza slipped the passkey into the slot above the handle and the light below the slot flashed solid green.

Carter and I were the first ones through the door. It was our job to handle the tall lady if she happened to be in there—and by "our job," I mean mostly *Carter's*—but thankfully no one was home.

"Nobody in the bedroom, either!" Ernie called out.

The suite clearly wasn't vacant, though. There were suitcases stacked in the living room and shopping bags strewn around the dining area. There were even a couple of black long-sleeved shirts draped over the backs of the couches.

A loud crunching sound had me whipping around toward the small kitchen. The Hungry Hippo was almost up to his waist in the tiny fridge, chowing down on what looked like a huge plate of cheesy nachos.

Sighing, I rolled my eyes. "This isn't the room, is it?"

"No, it is, Jorge! Dis is da room! Cross me heart!"

"Yeah, the room with a plate of unguarded nachos in the fridge, you nacho-loving fiend!"

"He's telling the truth, Jorge," said Ernie. "This is it. This is the treasure hunters' room."

I turned, getting ready to say, "How do you know?" but by the time I got halfway around, I had already spotted the answer to my question.

"And check this out," Liza said. In her hand was one of those long yellow notepads. And on the front page, written in fancy cursive, I saw this:

Cross the waters without a greedy hand.
Walk the path without a greedy eye.
Stab the heart of greed.
Offer a worthy sacrifice and seize the true treasure that lies before you!

La bruja's riddle, I suddenly realized. The dagger *and* the riddle!

But before I could shout "¡HEY, WACHA!" the door to the room clicked quietly open and a pair of familiar faces waltzed in. Or should I say, a pair of familiar oversized *biceps* . . .

CHAPTER 33

Up close and in the daytime, the acrobat twins looked even more buff than they had back in the museum. I mean, even their biceps had biceps. And probably their own zip codes, too!

The second they saw us, they froze dead in their tracks, staring blankly around for a moment like maybe they'd walked into the wrong room.

But they obviously hadn't walked into the wrong room. And after about five seconds, they figured that out. Which, sadly, left us with only one move...

"Bonjour, gentlemen!" I shouted in my cheeriest French accent—which, by the way, didn't sound very cheery or very French. "Pardone le intruzion, but we thought you'd be out a bit longer. Anyway, since you're back, we'll leave you alone and clean up some other time."

It was a decent bluff. I mean, c'mon, all four of us were even decked out in French maid outfits!

But apparently it wasn't good enough to fool the pair of circus twins, because their glaring eyes and clenching-and-unclenching fists were saying *We recognize you, punk. We recognize all of you!*

"Uh, guys?" I squeaked back at my buds. "A little help?"

Tearing off his maid's outfit, Carter sprang to my side, claws out, masses of dense brown fur sticking up like the quills of an angry porcupine. "I get them, Jorge!"

But the acrobat twins didn't so much as flinch! Instead, one of them went backflipping into the entryway closet and came front-flipping back out with a pair of gleaming pirate swords.

¡Santo cielos! These guys could move!

Then Wannabe Pirate Number One tossed a sword to Wannabe Pirate Number Two, who caught it in his meaty hand without even turning to look. Show-offs.

"Eh, I don't think I get them anymore, Jorge . . ." Carter said with a sheepish grin. The big guy had a phobia of sharp metal objects. It was almost as bad as my fear of being sliced in half.

So we organized a strategic retreat, hopping over the low leather couch to stand next to Liza and Ernie. Hey, like people say, *We're stronger together*, right?

"Everybody, grab a weapon!" shouted Liza, snatching up a decorative purple vase from an end table. I loved where her head was at! Only problem was, there weren't a whole lot of "weapons" lying around.

My eyes fell on a farm-fresh California orange on the coffee table, so I went with that. Yeah, totally embarrassing, I know. But at least it was better than what Ernie chose—which, in case you're wondering, was a pair of fluffy blue *throw pillows* from the love seat.

"Take this, you big bullies!" he cried, launching the pillows at the acrobats.

Two pirate swords flashed through the air and suddenly there were four pillows instead of two.

I stared at Ernie. "Dude, seriously?" But now it was *my* turn! And winding up like an MLB pitcher powering up a fastball, I launched my smooth citrusy grenade straight at Swole Bro Number Two—

Who—*¡híjole!*—caught it between his perfect, grinning teeth!

"Maybe we should run?" I suggested.

It turned out to be a very popular idea. We ran for our lives. Dodging between couches, jumping over living room furniture. The killer acrobats gave chase, slicing and dicing everything we tossed and toppled in their way.

My panicked eyes fell on an umbrella leaning against the kitchen counter. I instantly snatched it up and whirled around to face our attackers.

"EN GARDE!" I shouted.

Swole Bro Number One's lips split into a vicious grin. His sword whizzed inches from my nose.

The next thing I knew, I was holding *half* an umbrella.

Ernie, who was currently cowering behind me, squeaked, "Or not."

The deadly pirate sword swept up above our heads. We both shrieked in terror.

IT'S OVER! I thought.

But suddenly—

CHAPTER 34

"CHICA, CALL 911!" screamed Enrique, wrapping himself so tightly around Ernie's head that E-dog let out a yelp of pain.

"WHO DO YOU THINK I'M CALLING?" Liza already had her phone out and was dialing. "GHOST-BUSTERS?!"

There was a bloodcurdling *chop!* and all of a sudden, another pirate sword came slicing through the flimsy bathroom door in a deadly blur, this time passing so close to Carter's head that it actually sheared off about half an inch of fluffy fur!

"BUT I NO WANT A HAIRCUT!" cried the big guy, eyes jacked wide with terror.

"Ernie, help me!" I shouted. Over in the shower, it probably looked like I was doing pull-ups on the curtain rod, but what I was really trying to do was yank it free. It took two sets of hands and four straining arms to finish the job, but once we'd managed, I ran one end of the rod through the widest slash in the door, jabbing at the acrobats' sweaty, snarling faces with it, seeing if I could bop one on the nose, or at the very least distract them a little.

Liza, meanwhile, had gotten through to the police, and while she gave 911 the 411, she used an ironing board to—well, board up some of the slashes.

The next couple of seconds were a dizzy blur of chopping swords, flying wood, and panicking, screaming mouths. Then the sombrero shouted: "¡Esperen! Everybody stop! Hush! *Hush!*"

"What is it?!" I shrieked.

"LISTEN!"

So I did. "I don't hear anything."

"That's my point! I think the piratas made like pirate ships and sailed away!"

"Or they want us to *think* they sailed away!"

Just then, out in the main living area, we heard the bang of the room door as someone threw it open and then a half-familiar voice shouted, "Children! Where are you? It's Detective Sophia! Are you all right?"

¡Menos mal! We were saved! I flung open the bathroom door. "Hey! Yeah! We're in here! We're okay!"

The four of us scrambled out into the living room, where the detective was surveying the place with a look of stunned shock.

"Wow," she said, toeing the edge of a sliced-and-diced kitchen stool, "looks like you four did quite a remodel."

"It wasn't us!" I explained. "It was the thieves! The ones who robbed the *El Dorado* exhibit in the museum!"

To our right, a fresh gust blew in through the open balcony door, and I realized that the acrobat twins had probably escaped through there. They'd probably done synchronized backflips off the railing or something real showboat-y like that.

"My dad is innocent!" Ernie told the detective.

"Yeah, and we can prove it!" added Liza, holding out the famed Aztecan dagger.

"We found that right in this room! Right on that table over there!"

Suddenly Detective Sophia's eyes fixed on Enrique, and a human version of the shocked emoji basically spread across her face. "I see that wasn't all you found. *The missing sombrero.*"

Ernie grinned. "Yep, that's him!"

"It's the whole reason why the thieves are still in town," I explained as he handed Enrique over to her. "They've been going bananas looking for that hat! They think it's the last piece they need in order to discover the treasure of El Dorado."

The detective looked mighty impressed. And who could blame her? The five of us had single-handedly cracked the case! "But how did you three find it?"

"The sombrero sort of *called* to us," I said, and winked back at the gang.

"You children are simply incredible!" gushed Sophia. "You're really the most intrepid youngsters I've ever come across! I can't tell you how grateful I am to you three. There really are no words. We owe you *everything*."

"Just doing our civic duty, ma'am," I said as humbly as I could manage (which, by the way, wasn't very).

Detective Sophia flashed me a grin so wide that it put most other grins to shame. "And it's incredibly appreciated!" Then she barked, "Now tie these children up and let's get ready to move!"

"Yes!" I wholeheartedly agreed. "Tie us up and let's—"

Hold up. What did she just say?

"Uh, can you repeat that?" I said.

But she didn't have to. Because not two seconds later, the pair of acrobat pirate wannabes swaggered out of the closet next to the exit door, grinning identical evil grins.

CHAPTER 35

"HEY, THAT'S THEM!" shouted Ernie. "Those are two of the treasure hunters! Arrest them!"

Liza and I both turned to him with looks that said, *Hello?* "I think she knows, Ernie," Liza pointed out.

I saw Ernie's entire face collapse into a disappointed frown. "Oh. Right."

"But I don't get it!" I said. "You're betraying your badge and partner?"

Detective Sophia didn't answer; instead she glanced casually over at the two acrobat losers who had lined up, one in front of the other, like they were getting ready to perform some big aerial trick.

Then they did perform a trick. Only it wasn't the kind of trick I'd expected.

Once his moustache was in place, the realization came crashing over me like I'd just been slimed on Nickelodeon: She hadn't betrayed her partner—he was standing right in front of us! And *he* was actually *they*!

"Oh my gosh, you're the third treasure-hunting circus clown!" I gasped, turning back to "Detective" Sophia. "And *none* of you are actually detectives!" They'd all just been playing the part so they could run around town asking questions to whoever they wanted and not draw any attention.

It was so twisted it was almost genius!

"And it looks like you three are a bit slow," said the acrobat on top, with a grin so big it made his giant moustache come unglued at the corner.

But believe it or not, that wasn't even the silliest part. That award goes to the dude's *voice*! It was so high and thin and squeaky that you'd think he was part mouse!

"Hey, dat big guy got a funny voice," Carter giggled, and I had to clap a hand over my mouth just to not laugh in the dude's face!

"It ain't our faults!" the one on the bottom roared—well, more like *squeaked*. "Do you have any idea what swallowing a flaming sword for two performances a week can do to your vocal cords?!"

Beside me, Liza smacked her hands together in frustration. "Of course!" she whispered, glaring up at the tall blue-eyed lady. "Zofia is Sophia in Polish! It was staring us in the face the whole time!"

Not five feet away, though, I saw the edges of the ringleader's lips curl into an evil Cheshire cat grin. "Bardzo dobry!" she said, and laughed. "Bravo!"

At that point, Enrique obviously couldn't take it anymore, because he quit playing the part of an inanimate object and began flopping violently around in the lady's hand. "¡Suéltame! Let go! Get your greedy paws off me!"

"Ah, the screaming sombrero..." whispered Zofia in a tone of hushed wonder. "And it speaks! Just like the legends say!"

The Swole Bros, meanwhile, were both gaping at Enrique as if they'd never seen a talking hat before. Where had those two been living—under a rock?

"That's right," said Enrique. "And if you don't put me down *ahora mismo*, you're gonna be hearing me speak *loud and clear!*"

"Ha! Well played!" Zofia told the sombrero. "You

quite surprised and confused us that day in the museum. A word of warning, though—if I hear even the *tiniest* scream out of you, I'm turning you into the world's oldest leather visor."

If a sombrero could cross its arms and turn smugly away from someone, Enrique did right then. "You don't deserve to handle such exquisite beauty," he grumbled at her.

The fake detective just grinned evilly in return. "I'm glad we understand each other. Now, as for you, my dear children, you will be coming with us."

"What? No way!" I shouted. "We're not going anywhere with you people!"

"You either come with us alive or you stay here *not* so alive," said Zofia, thumbing back the hammer of a crusty old pirate pistol as she slipped it smoothly out of her coat.

Well, if she put it like that... "In that case, I think we will be joining you after all."

One of the acrobats leveled the razor edge of his pirate sword on Carter. "What are we going to do about the big kid in the dog costume?" he asked Zofia.

"That's not a dog costume. That's a—" Mrs. Blackbeard's cold green eyes sort of crossed for a sec, then she glanced at me with a look of total bewilderment. "What in the world is that thing?"

"It's a chupacabra," I explained. "And it's more birthday suit than costume."

"Nice try." The other acrobat grinned at me like he thought I was making some kind of joke. "We remember him from the club last night. He's got some nice moves."

Carter bowed his head in a small thank-you. "Gracias." Then, thinking quick I guess, he shouted, "Jorge! I go get help!" and suddenly whirled, making a break for the balcony.

It was a decent try. I mean, it *could've* worked.

But not with these circus villains. Zofia, the fourth-generation aerialist and trained marksman, had the reflexes of a jungle cat. Before Carter had even taken two steps toward the open door, she'd already swung the pirate hand-cannon toward him and was shouting "*Stop!*"

But I knew Carter wouldn't stop. He'd happily risk himself to save us.

And I knew what that meant Zofia would do.

In that moment, my blood froze.

My brain froze.

Everything in me just *froze*.

But somehow the rest of me leapt into action!

Without thinking, I snatched up the small metal coffee table next to the couch and, using it like Captain America's famous shield, dove in front of Carter just as a huge blast of sound slammed painfully against my ears.

The impact of whatever had exploded out of that crusty old thing was pretty gnarly.

It didn't just bang off the thick aluminum top of the coffee table—it smashed into it like a crashing meteor!

The incredible force sent me hurtling back into Carter and sent the chupacabra fumbling backward on his bony heels.

Our momentum carried us through the open sliding glass door and all the way out to the iron railing of the little balcony—

And then—*¡Dios mío!*—*over it*!

CHAPTER 36

You think about the most random stuff when you're plummeting to your death.

For me, I thought about how I'd ended up in Boca Falls, New Mexico. How my mom had sent me out here to live with my grandparents so that I could have what she'd called "a normal, stable life." I remembered her promising me that I wouldn't ever get bored in Boca.

Well, at least she'd been right about that part...

Squeezing my eyes shut, I braced myself for a loud *SPLAT!* followed by a long and very quiet nap.

Only the *SPLAT!* never came. What actually came was a ginormous *SPLASH!* as Carter and I basically belly flopped into the deep end of the motel's giant swimming pool!

The splash landing was definitely a relief. Better

than a crash landing, that's for sure. But it wasn't by any means a *soft* landing.

The jolt of the collision knocked the breath out of my lungs, slapped the sense out of my cabeza, and left me dizzy and disoriented as I sank like a stone toward the glittering blue-tiled bottom of the pool.

For a moment everything happened slowly—like I was dreaming it. My head ached something fierce, and I actually began to feel a little sleepy.

But next thing I knew, Carter's huge furry hands were dragging me out of the chlorine-scented water like a heavy sack of rice while I wheezed and choked and gasped, trying desperately to suck air into my pancaked chest.

We collapsed onto a pair of plastic lounge chairs and started coughing up enough water to fill an inflatable swimming pool.

"You hurt, Jorge?" I heard the big guy ask, patting me gently on the back like a mom burping a newborn.

"Never felt wetter!" I joked. Honestly, I was just grateful that the wannabe pirates had picked a room with a pool view.

A moment later, a small breathless voice behind us gasped, "Hey! You guys okay?"

I looked around. Three freckle-faced kids with eyes so wide they could've doubled as softballs were standing behind us beneath the shade of a nearby umbrella.

They all had big globs of sunscreen smeared over their noses and big Avengers-themed floaties on their arms.

My lungs were still burning, still begging for oxygen, so I just gave them a big thumbs-up.

Then one of the kids asked, "Is that your monster?"

"What monster?!" I managed to choke out.

The dripping end of a chubby finger was pointing over my shoulder at Carter.

"Oh, *him*. No, that's my professionally trained high-diving dog," I said. "We were just practicing our tandem dive—" I got that far and not another word before all the events of the last sixty seconds came slamming back into me kind of the way Zofia's three-hundred-year-old lead ball had slammed into the coffee table—

Liza and Ernie!

They were still up there!

Up there with those pirates!

CHAPTER 37

With Carter doing his best Lassie impersonation, the two of us rushed back into the hotel and ran right up to the front desk, Carter "barking" and me shouting, "*Somebody call 911!*"

But no sooner had those words come flying out of my mouth than two police officers in uniform rushed in through the main entrance, shoulder radios crackling.

"Officers!" I shouted. "There are pirates on the fifth floor! I mean, *bad guys!*"

I explained everything to them on the elevator ride up. But the second they kicked in the door to room 502, I had even more explaining to do.

The room was empty.

No fake detective lady.

No wannabe pirates.

No Liza.

No Ernie.

No one!

But even more cabeza-blowing, the place was neat as a pin! All the furniture had been stood up and straightened out, and even the bathroom looked okay. Well, the door was missing but everything else was fine.

"Prank calling 911 is a *crime*," said one of the officers, glaring at me with an annoyed look. "You can get in serious trouble for that."

"But I didn't prank call anybody!" I tried to explain. "I wasn't even the one who called you in the first place! That was my friend Liza. Who, by the way, has just been kidnapped!"

The other cop looked even more annoyed than his partner. "You said they tore the place up with pirate swords. Doesn't look torn up to me."

For several seconds I was too confused to answer. I felt like I'd stumbled into some parallel universe where we *hadn't* discovered those circus clowns' secret hideout, hadn't found the ancient Aztecan dagger, and *hadn't* hidden in the bathroom while the two pirate wannabes tried to hack their way through the door with swords. But what had actually happened was pretty obvious.

"They cleaned up the scene of the crime!" I shouted. "To cover their tracks! They're criminal masterminds, I tell you!"

Suddenly, there was a sharp crackle from one of the officers' shoulder radios, and a staticky voice on the other end said: "Calling all available units! Huge mess at the intersection of Salvia Avenue and Main Street! A vehicle sped out of the parking lot of the Château Blanche, running several red lights and causing multiple collisions."

"That's them!" I screamed. "Making their getaway!"

Neither of the cops looked awfully convinced, though. On the way out of the room, the shorter one turned to me and said, "Next time you prank call 911, we're telling your parents."

Then they were gone.

CHAPTER 38

The situation was turning out worse than a batch of my grandma's chicken empanadas. Not only had a gang of treasure-hunting thieves kidnapped two of my best friends (and the world's biggest-mouthed sombrero), there wasn't a law enforcement officer in Boca Falls who would believe me!

Worse, when Carter tried to track Liza's and Ernie's scents through the hotel, we wound up in the parking lot, standing in an empty parking space where those Pirates of the Caribbean jerks had probably stuck Liza and Ernie in their musty, claustrophobic trunk and driven off.

Beyond frustrated, I spun around and kicked a rock across the sidewalk. "Now what? Who's going to help us find Liza and Ernie? And where would we even start looking?"

"Jorge, da treasure hunters goin' after *the treasure*. So if we find the treasure, we find Liza and Ernie!"

"Well, yeah. But you're looking at this whole thing upside down! Finding the treasure of El Dorado would be even *harder* than finding Liza and Ernie. I mean, how are we supposed to find some legendary, never-before-discovered Aztecan treasure that's remained hidden for the last thousand years—in the next couple of hours?"

"Easy," Carter said with a shrug. "'Cause I know where it is."

Honestly? I couldn't have been more surprised if Carter had whipped out a lightsaber and sliced the RESERVED PARKING sign in half. "Hold your caballos. You're telling me that you know where *the* treasure of El Dorado is? How . . . I mean, *HOW*?"

"'Cause Enrique tole me. He da real map!"

I blinked. "He's the real what?"

"Map! He the only one who know da secret location of El Dorado. He tole me dat's part of his curse. The witch tole him dat he gonna stay a sombrero until he finds somebody with a pure heart who will give the treasure back to the descendants of da people she took it from. She wanted to teach those people a lesson. But she say the treasure still belong to their families. Enrique tole me dat he been looking for somebody pure of heart all dis time!"

"And he ... uh ... chose *you*?"

Carter gave a small shrug. "I guess. Oh, and it took him so long because he say he gotta be one hundred percent sure the person he tell about da treasure is pure of heart, because if dey keep da treasure for demselves, his curse will get even WORSE!"

"Really? Worse than spending the rest of his life as a crummy old sombrero? What could be worse than that?"

Everyone's favorite bloodsucker slapped on his thinking cap for a sec. "Being stuck as a goat, maybe?"

Hmm. I could see that. Especially with a hungry Carter sniffing around. "Wow. So Enrique basically just poured his heart out to you, huh?"

"Oh, no, he don't have a heart, Jorge. No blood either. Mostly just thread and goat leather." The chupacabra's voice dropped real low all of a sudden, like he was telling the world's greatest secret: "Trust me, I checked."

CHAPTER 39

According to what Enrique had told Carter, the legendary treasure of El Dorado was buried deep within the heart of Las Tres Hermanas mountains, also known as the Three Sisters.

And according to Google Maps, that mountain range was located in the Chihuahuan Desert of southwestern New Mexico.

The way I saw things, it didn't really matter whether the treasure was actually hidden there or not. All that mattered was that *Enrique* believed it was, so when the circus clowns eventually pried it out of him (which they would, because all they'd really have to do was threaten to scuff up his beloved brim a little), that's where they'd take Liza and Ernie.

Our main problem? The Three Sisters was *far* and no one with a car was going to believe our ridiculous story enough to drive us all the way out to a rural stretch of coyote-infested desert. So I improvised. I decided to teach the chupacabra how to ride my bike.

CHUPACARTER AND THE SCREAMING SOMBRERO

We reached a shadowy crack in the base of the middle hermana—a gap in the rock just wide enough for us to squeeze our way into.

"How'd you spot this from all the way back there?!" I asked Carter.

To which he replied, with his trademark fangy grin: "I'm a chupacabra, 'member?"

The passageway into the mountain was nearly pitch-black, with only a faint faraway glow of purplish moonbeams lighting our way. The ground was rough and the walls were even rougher, jagged and craggy, with stony shards sharp enough to snag my clothes (and Carter's fur).

As we wormed our way through the tiny space

hanging with ancient spiderwebs and littered with the bony remains of long-dead critters, my heart was pounding out a steady *Get me out of here!* rhythm.

But I gritted my teeth and forced myself to stay calm. Forced myself to think about my friends—Liza, Ernie, and even Enrique—who were the whole reason we were creeping around down here in the first place.

After what felt like *forever*, the tunnel suddenly opened up and we found ourselves standing in a vast underground cavern about the size of a baseball field.

Masses of jagged stalactites reached down from the domed ceiling like chupacabra fangs, and the walls were some kind of crystallized volcanic rock that glistened as if freshly wet. Which made perfect sense, since the cavern was split right down the middle by an enormous underground lake.

As the cone of my flashlight beam played over the surface of the rippling water, I noticed that it sparkled strangely, in hues of silvers and blacks and blues, and that there was absolutely no way to walk around it.

Frowning, I turned to Carter. "What do we do now?"

"Swim?"

"That's what I was thinking. Only I forgot my trunks."

No. There had to be an easier way. Turning on my heel, I swept my flashlight carefully back and forth over the gleaming walls of the cave, looking for another tunnel, a secret set of steps carved into the crystal—something, *anything* to help us get across. But there was nothing.

I had just opened my mouth to say that maybe we'd taken a wrong turn at the rat skeleton a few yards back when the padded fingers of my fanged buddy suddenly gripped my bicep.

"Jorge, ¡mira!" he hissed.

So I looked—

And gaped.

At a boat.

A shiny green-and-yellow rowboat bobbing quietly on the shore of the lake. The *near* shore.

How could I have missed that? I wondered, feeling sort of dazed.

Then I realized that I *couldn't* have. There was just no way! The boat was straight dead ahead and about as obvious as—well, a rowboat floating on the shore of an empty lake.

Pretty sure my eyes were playing tricks on me, I tried to blink the hallucination away, but it refused to skedaddle.

"That... wasn't there before," I whispered uneasily. *"Was it?"*

The large, owllike eyes of the chupacabra blinked once, twice, three times as he shook his giant, furry head. "No... no estaba."

"But—*how*?"

Carter was totally silent for several moments. His pooch-like nostrils widened as he sniffed the cool air that blew off the surface of the strange, shimmering lake.

"Magic," he said finally—*ominously*. "I can smell it."

CHAPTER 40

I'll be the first to admit that I wasn't super excited about the prospect of riding a spontaneously materializing ghost boat across a creepy subterranean lake in the middle of this midnight mountain world. But since there apparently was no ferry service in the area and I'd left my personal Jet Ski in the pocket of my *other* shorts, I recited a silent little prayer and climbed warily aboard.

And you want to hear the freakiest part? We didn't even have to push off! The second our butts hit the stiff wooden seats, the boat jerked into motion, setting off on a steady course across the glimmering lake. Carter and I looked at each other like, *Is this really happening?* and all I could do was shake my head. Honestly, the whole thing reminded me of a theme park ride where an attendant controls the boats from a tiny closet just out of sight.

Only I didn't even want to think about who might be controlling *this* particular boat.

We were halfway across the lake when something in the water caught my eye. A bright, glinting something. Down near the murky bottom of the mountain lake. And that's when I realized what it was—

Coins!

LEGIT GOLD COINS!

Dozens and dozens and dozens of them—maybe hundreds!—carved with intricate geometric patterns and scattered across the lake bottom like stars across the night sky.

Then I realized something else. This lake wasn't actually that deep. As a matter of fact, I was pretty sure I could grab a coin by simply reaching over the side of the boat.

And can you *imagine* how many Xbox games I could buy with just one of those coins? I could walk into any video game store in the world and practically clean the place out!

Suddenly, I had to have one. No, not just one. Why

one? Why not *all* of them? Every single coin I could get my hands on! Every single coin in this entire la—

"*JORGE, NO!*"

A shout, loud and frantic, broke the spell.

I blinked, coming out of a trance, and realized with a jolt that I'd been leaning out over the side of the rowboat, reaching dreamily toward the water with both hands.

Now Carter pulled me back into the boat, where I sat blinking dazedly up at him.

"No toques, Jorge," he warned me, shaking his head gravely. "Remember what the witch's riddle say: 'Cross the lake without a greedy hand.'"

There was a small twig on the floor of the boat. With two clawed fingers, Carter picked it up and dipped the thorny tip carefully into the silvery water.

Immediately I heard a sizzling, popping sound and saw wisps of grayish steam curl up around his fingers as the section of the twig he'd dipped in the water began to slowly dissolve.

¡Dios mío! That could've been my hand!

"It's like acid or something!" I shrieked.

Carter nodded grimly. "I thought I smelled something funny in there. Is magia."

Suddenly the rowboat that rowed itself shuddered, and I saw that we had reached the opposite shore. Clumps of thorny weeds, their leaves black with soot, grew wild out of the rocky soil.

"Get me off this thing," I said, already climbing out. "And watch out for those thorns. I don't even want to imagine what might happen if you get pricked by one of those..."

CHAPTER 41

A narrow, craggy passageway led us deeper into the mountain. All around us, getting stuck to our hands and faces, hung the sticky, dusty webs of giant spiders I really hoped we wouldn't get to meet. The cave walls loomed impossibly high and impossibly dark. They were the most impressive walls we'd seen yet, because these were carved with jaw-dropping designs—what I guessed were Aztecan pictograms: jaguar and eagle heads, two-headed serpents, warriors, kings, and dancing monkeys. It was all so incredibly cool.

"I feel like a Mexican Indiana Jones right now!" I admitted, trailing my fingertips over the heads of howling wolves. "I wonder what it says."

"It tells the story of a witch who robbed a king,"

replied Carter, his mismatched eyes slowly scanning the wall. "Seven kings."

And now that he'd explained it, I could *almost* see it—a creepily familiar scene sketched out in the cold, dry rock before our eyes: the tale of an ancient bruja who had plundered seven golden cities. The exact story that Ernie had told us. The *true* story of El Dorado.

"Hold up," I said. "You read ancient Nahuatl?"

"Uh-huh. It's like a second cousin to chupacabra language."

I gawked. "You peeps have your own language?"

Carter looked at me like I had as many brain cells as a Big Mac. "Everybody got dey own language, Jorge. How else they supposed to talk to each other?"

I was about to ask him what other secrets he'd been keeping from me when I saw the pointy tips of his long ears begin to twitch like fur-covered satellite dishes.

He hissed, "¿Oíste eso? I think is Enrique!"

Silent as ninjas, we crept along the curving passageway on our tippy-toes for maybe fifty yards, then squatted way down low, peering around the rocky wall—

"I hate this place!" cried a very familiar, very *annoying* voice—Enrique! This might've been the first time I was actually thrilled to hear the ole brim flapper! "Only terrible things have happened to me in here! You are horrible people! Horrible, *despicable* people! Just look what you did to that kindhearted creature and the boy with the giant head!"

The boy with the giant head? He'd better not be talking about me...

Señor Sombrero wasn't through with his tongue-lashing. "If I had legs, I would kick you! If I had fingers, I would poke you! If I had a chef's cooking kit complete with a metal spatula, I would—"

"SILENCE!" exploded Zofia. "If I hear another complaint out of you—just *one*—I'm going to drag you back to that cursed lake and drop you to the bottom with a boulder slung around your brim!" Then, with another impatient glance down at her watch, she shouted, "Piotr, *please* finish bandaging his hand already, and let's move! We've wasted enough time!"

"His hand needs medical attention," Liza snapped, jumping to her feet. "The stuff in that lake could've been some undiscovered form of sulfuric acid. He could have third-degree burns!"

"I said *SILENCE!*" roared the circus lady, trembling with barely controlled fury as she glared at Liza. "If I hear one more peep out of any of you, *you'll* be the ones needing medical attention!"

With an irritated huff, Liza sat back down. Behind her, the injured acrobat dude gasped and gritted his teeth as his twin poured water on his wounded hand from a metal canteen.

Sliding back into cover, I hissed, "What do we do?"

"We pretend dey goats!" whispered Carter. "And go sneaky sneak!"

"Pretend they're *what*? What's that supposed to mea—" Then it hit me. "Oh! You mean the *sneak up behind them* part..."

The chupacabra's fangs flashed in the dark. "Uh-huh!"

"I love the way you think, amigo! Okay, let's rock and roll!"

Carter and I drew up a quick play, then, summoning our inner Batmans, began to sneak our way closer, sticking tight to the shadows. The stony ground muffled the sound of our tiptoeing feet as we darted from stalagmite to stalagmite, always keeping

CHUPACARTER AND THE SCREAMING SOMBRERO

low, and once we'd made it to within five or so yards of the Cirque du Villains, it was baddie beatdown time.

Carter and I slipped silently out of the deep shadows, and I crept up behind Zofia on my tiptoes with my baseball bat gripped tightly in both hands.

I tapped her on the shoulder. "¡Hola, amigos!"

Then, as she whirled in surprise—

At the same moment, Carter pounced on the pair of pirate swords lying on the ground near the acrobat twins, snatching them up in his clawed hands.

"Did you miss us?" I asked Zofia. The glaring green eyes of the clown lady narrowed on me, and she hissed like an angry cat at the dog pound. I guess the answer was no.

"Well, how about you guys?" I asked Liza and Ernie. But even those two let out shrieks that could have woken the dead!

"*WHAT IS IT?!*" I screamed. "*WHAT HAPPENED?*"

"*G-G-GHOSTS!*" was Ernie's answer. Worse, he was pointing a trembling, dirt-smudged finger straight at moi!

Fortunately, Liza saved me the effort and cut him an annoyed sideways glare. "Ghosts, Ernie? Seriously?"

"That was the first thing that popped into my head, too," admitted Enrique. "Not gonna lie!"

"Guys, Carter and I didn't plunge to our *deaths* back at the hotel," I explained with a groan. "We plunged into the hotel pool."

And suddenly, all the color that had gone rushing out of Ernie's face a moment ago now came rushing back in, and he leapt to his feet, shouting: "Oh my gosh, so you're both really alive?"

"Uh, obviously, Ernie!"

E-dog let out the world's biggest sigh of relief. "Oh man, Jorge! You have no idea how happy it makes me to hear that!"

Liza sighed. "Talk about a couple of empty hats..."

"Liza, call your dad!" I shouted. "Tell him to come get us and bring the cavalry!"

"Already tried, Jorge! First chance I got when they brought us in here!" Liza dug her phone out of her pocket as Zofia grumbled something about her being a sneaky brat. "But I'm getting ZERO bars! I even texted 911, but I don't think that's going to go through either."

I should've known it wasn't going to be that easy. I mean, what in my life ever was?

"No biggie. Plan B, then. Let's just go back the way we came, and we'll call your dad when we get back outside."

"You can't go back, cactus brain!" shouted Zofia, jabbing her torch in my direction. "Once you've entered la bruja's mountain, the only way out is to complete the challenges! Don't you know anything about the legends?"

Panic squeezed my insides as my gaze shifted to Ernie. "Please tell me that isn't true."

He gave a small shrug. "I can say it's not true, but then I'd be lying."

"She's right," agreed Enrique. "Once started, the challenge must be completed. Believe me, I hate it more than anyone, but it's the truth. The only way out now is to use la bruja's riddle to complete her four tests."

¡Fantástico! Like I said—never easy.

I guess there was only one way out of this mountain tomb, and that—unfortunately—was by going farther in.

CHAPTER 42

The flickering orange light of Zofia's torch lit our way as we plunged deeper and deeper into the dark heart of the mountain. The funny thing was, now that we had the numbers on our side, Ernie had gone from terrified prisoner to overly chatty tour guide, excitedly whipping his flashlight this way and that as he told us everything we ever wanted to know—and plenty we *didn't*—about the famous Three Sisters mountain range.

"The north peak is the tallest, and I'm guessing that's the one we're currently underneath. Supposedly all three mountains were named after the daughters of the wealthy miner who used to own these lands way back when. I think I read once that their names were Alice, Kate, and Lou, but don't quote me on that."

"And what did the miner name the secret exit, and where can we find it?" I couldn't help but joke.

Ernie gave me a sideways smirk, then continued with the tour. "Anyway, back in the early 1900s, a whole mess of prospectors believed there was hidden treasure buried somewhere in these mountains. Supposedly tons of silver ingots. But I don't think anyone would have guessed that this was the secret location of the El Dorado treasure!"

"You know what I just realized?" Liza said as we ducked into another dank and drippy tunnel. "If you three had framed pretty much anyone but Ernie's dad, you might have actually gotten away with this."

"You don't say," grumbled Zofia.

"So why'd you do it?" I asked, sort of curious. "What'd Mr. Nez ever do to you?"

If looks could bite, the one the circus lady tossed my way right then would've taken a T. rex–size chunk out of my heinie.

"Nothing!" she snapped. "We've never even met the man! He was simply a means to an end. When we failed to acquire the sombrero on our first break-in, we were forced to stick around. But we needed a way to get the police out of our hair, and Mr. Nez was that way."

"Basically you framed an innocent man," I said with disgust. "What a bunch of scallywags."

We walked on through the mountain gloom as the air grew cold and the stony ground became all loose and crunchy. The place smelled funny, too, like an ancient burial tomb where all the mummies had spent the last three thousand or so years cutting mad cheese.

A few moments later, as we continued along the narrow gravelly path, a bony finger poked me in the ribs. Then the owner of that finger (Carter, in case you were wondering) rasped, "Jorge, ¡mira! Look!"

He was pointing up ahead, way off into the deep dark, where, suddenly, spectacularly, stars had begun to twinkle to life. Wait. No—not stars...*gems*! Pulsing bluish-yellow gems, easily the size of my fist! The cave walls must've been loaded with them!

"The treasure of El Dorado!" cried Mini-Hulk Number Two, pointing with his bandage-wrapped hand like the first kid in the park who spots the ice cream truck. "There it is!"

"That is *not* the treasure," Zofia said firmly. "It's *a*

test. You know the witch's warning. 'Walk the path without a greedy eye.'"

But the thief was already running! Already racing out toward the glimmering gems!

"Don't fear, Zofia!" he shouted back. "I'll retrieve the treasure for us!"

"PIOTR, STOP!" she screamed. But even before the words were fully out of her mouth, the treasure-loving acrobat suddenly vanished! Into thin air—like he'd stepped off the edge of a cliff!

It all happened so fast we only heard him scream for maybe a split second, and then—

Silence.

There was a loud clang of metal as Carter dropped the pirate swords to cover his eyes with both furry paws. On Ernie's head, Enrique let out a horror-movie-worthy shriek while Liza cried, "Somebody do something!"

Little did she know that somebody *was* doing something.

Quick as a cobra, Zofia snatched up the two pirate swords Carter had dropped, tossing one to the remaining acrobat.

"Hey, that's not fair!" shouted Ernie.

Zofia raised her sword threateningly. "What about any of your dealings with us makes you think we play by the rules?"

"But aren't you even going to try to help your friend?" I yelled.

"I already tried!" snarled Zofia. "But he refused to heed the witch's warnings! Now *move!*" she said, urging us up the path with the business end of her pirate espada.

"But . . . *Piotr*," murmured the remaining acrobat twin, still looking shocked and totally terrified by what had happened to his twin. "What about Piotr?"

"There is nothing we can do for him now, Jan," answered Zofia coldly. "Perhaps when the challenge is complete and the curse broken, we will try to find him. But right now we have treasure to find."

CHAPTER 43

About sixty or so yards down the path, we found ourselves standing in the middle of a large, rocky platform that jutted out seemingly over nothing.

In the darkness up ahead, I could just make out a sturdy-looking rope bridge that drooped across the black abyss like a saggy clothesline.

It was nice to see.

But even nicer?

It led to an opening!

Finally! Maybe a way out of this place! I thought.

What *wasn't* so nice to see, however—what made my insides shrivel up like fried pork rinds and turned my blood to ice—was what was swinging just *inches* above that bridge.

Hmm.

How should I describe them?
Well, maybe you should just see for yourself...

The moment Enrique got a look at the maze of giant swinging scalpels, he let out a piercing, bloodcurdling shriek of horror, which perfectly summed up my feelings on the matter, too.

"The third and final obstacle," murmured Zofia, as if in a trance. "Behold! Our destiny awaits!"

"Our *destiny*?" I snapped. "With who? The Grim Reaper?!"

"Don't be a coward, child! We have arrived at the witch's final challenge."

"That's not a challenge!" Liza shouted. "That's an impossibility! And the only destiny waiting for you through that forest of swinging scalpels is being sliced into five million pieces!"

"What does la bruja's riddle say about this obstacle?" I asked Ernie, and he quoted it for me, word for word.

"'Stab the heart. Offer a worthy sacrifice and seize the true treasure before it's too late.'"

"The heart must lie on the other side," whispered Mr. Buff Acrobat Dude.

"Jan, you have trained all your life for this moment," said the pirate lady. "Do you think you can do it?"

Jan was dead silent for several seconds. Then, gathering his courage, I guess, he said, "There isn't an obstacle course in this world that can keep us from the treasure."

"You're not actually going to try to cross that bridge, are you?!" I screamed. "You'll be carved up worse than a turkey at my grandma's Thanksgiving! And that woman *loves* turkey!"

"We couldn't turn back now even if we wanted to," said Zofia icily, her gazed fixed on the swinging blades of death. "The witch's challenges must be completed. The only way out now is to reach the other side, find the heart, then stab it."

"You do realize that even if he somehow manages to make it across, that doesn't mean any of *us* will be able to. So stab the heart and then what?"

"We'll cross that proverbial bridge after we cross this literal one."

After a few quick full-body stretches, the acrobat twin was ready to roll—or should I say, ready to be sliced and diced. Zofia said, "Godspeed, Jan!" and he was off.

I immediately spun to face the other way. "I can't watch this. I can't handle blood!"

"Me neither!" said Carter, turning with me.

Liza, Ernie, Enrique, and I all gave him a *You're kidding, right?* look, and the chupacabra grinned sheepishly. "Unless I drinkin' it, of course."

"¡OYE!" cried Enrique from the top of Ernie's head. "That was a close one! A blade almost sliced that guy in half."

I clamped my hands over my ears. "I'm not listening! Not listening! Falalalalalalalala!"

Exactly three minutes later, I heard Liza say, "He's done, Jorge," and my insides twisted up like a pretzel.

"*He's dead?*" I burst out.

Liza smacked me with an eye roll. "Not dead—*done*. He couldn't make it past the third blade."

"It's impossible!" cried Jan, panting heavily as he bumbled this way. His shirt and cargo pants were so in tatters that it looked like they'd been washed in a blender. "There's no way through! *None!* Too many blades, and they're too fast!"

"Thank you!" I said, throwing my hands up in exasperation. I mean, it didn't take a genius to figure that out.

"It would take a superhuman effort," he gasped to Zofia. "Nothing less."

Suddenly an evil little smile began to creep its way across her thin, pale lips. I didn't like that smile. It was basically bad news in smile form.

"In that case," she said, turning her gaze on Carter, "good thing we have someone here who isn't human at all."

CHAPTER 44

"He's human!" I shouted. "That's just a costume!"

The Wicked Witch of the Caribbean made a face. "Do I look like a fool to you? He's obviously a chupacabra! Just like you said before!"

"But if you really believe he's a chupacabra, then how come you're not freaking out?"

"I've worked in circuses all my life, child. I've seen *much* weirder." Her gaze flicked over to Enrique. "And after meeting a talking hat, a talking cryptid isn't quite so outlandish."

Eh. She had point.

"Enough wasting time!" shouted Zofia. "Cross the bridge, beast!"

"You leave that big lovable furball out of this!" growled Enrique. "¿Me oíste? He's got nothing to do with your twisted love of treasure! He doesn't even *care* about treasure!"

"Yeah!" Ernie chipped in. "And he's not just some *beast*—he's our friend!"

"In that case, I give you a choice, monster. Save your friends or save yourself." Pirate Lady's right arm rose, leveling the razor-sharp point of her sword at Carter's skinny neck.

The chupacabra immediately retreated back a step. "I no like swords."

"Neither do I, if you want to know the truth. But your friends here will soon like them even less. Because every minute you stand there *not* attempting to reach the other side, it will cost you one friend. Whom shall I begin with? Hmm . . . perhaps the Dodgers fan? I've always been a Pirates fan myself," she mused, aiming her sword between my eyes as I tried not to pee my pants.

"No, don't hurt dem!" Carter begged. "I . . . I try it, okay? I try."

Zofia grinned evilly. "You have a deal, monster."

Looking like a scolded puppy, Carter started reluctantly for the edge of the platform—toward the bridge and the swinging pendulum knives. But when we went to join him, Captain Heartless blocked us, raising the deadly blade of her sword in our faces.

"You four watch from here," she ordered. "Wouldn't want you to distract your friend."

"This I definitely can't watch!" I turned back to face the opposite way.

Several tense moments passed. Then, out of nowhere, Enrique let out this gut-twisting screech that made my heart jump halfway to Honolulu!

"What happened?!" I screamed. "Did Carter get hurt?!"

"What? No," said Enrique. "He still hasn't started. I thought I saw a bat."

"A *bat*?" I nearly smacked the leather off of Enrique's "face" right then and there!

But the next moment my eyes flew involuntarily to Carter, who was standing at the edge of the stony platform and staring back at us with big puppy dog eyes.

I watched him suck in a deep, slow breath, like he was trying to muster all his courage as he turned to face the obstacle course of death.

Then, next thing I knew, the chupacabra was off.

CHAPTER 45

Even though I didn't want to watch, my eyes were superglued on my best friend. Carter sprang forward, lunging past the hissing arc of the first blade and diving into a headfirst roll in order to dodge the second.

He came up on one knee inches from blade number three, trying to gauge its sickening speed as the deadly thing slashed by his face close enough to stir the fur around his ears. He was far enough out along the rope bridge now that his slim, Chester the Cheetah–like body was becoming lost in the wisps of grayish fog that rose from the chasm. But it really didn't make much of a difference to me, because I honestly couldn't take anymore!

This is so unfair! I screamed on the inside as I tore my eyes away from him. *And it's so completely pigheaded!*

I mean, was a pile of treasure really worth all this? Was it really worth the life of a living thing—who happened to be my best friend? Of course not! No amount of treasure was.

And that's because, I realized right then, life and friendship—or let's call it *love*, since I admit I love my friends and my mom and my grandparents—are the greatest treasures of all. Nothing else in this whole wide world could even come close.

As I started pacing back and forth on the hard stone, angrily kicking up clouds of ancient dirt and dust, I couldn't help but feeling that something just wasn't adding up here.

Seriously—what did "stab the heart of greed" have to do with getting across that forest of swinging death? Nothing that I could see. And it didn't seem to me like it was something the witch would have set up as a challenge, either. Up to now, all her challenges had been tests of morality—tests to see if we could keep our greed in check. But now she was throwing the world's deadliest obstacle course at us? It didn't fit.

I closed my eyes.

Think, Jorge. Think!

What were we missing?

The heart of greed. Stab the heart of greed.

It was all about the heart... But where were we supposed to find a heart down here?

I couldn't figure it out. You want to hear the funniest part, though? When I opened my eyes again, I was starting to see "hearts" everywhere. I mean, this entire stony platform, if you looked at it as a whole, was more or less heart shaped. Heck, even the tiles in the stone (especially now that my stomping feet had cleared away the top layer of the grime) formed a sort of abstract heart-shaped mosaic that even had a reddish color to it—

No way...

Could it really be?

All of a sudden, a few yards behind me, the breathless, panicked voice of Carter rang out in the hollowness of the huge chamber.

"¡No es posible!" he cried. "Halfway across, da bridge *vanishes*! It missing a HUGE piece!"

I instantly spun around to look. Carter was back! And even better, in one piece! Sure, a few patches of his shaggy, curly coat looked like they'd gotten into a wrestling match with a high-powered lawn mower, but everything important was still firmly attached!

"Try again, monster!" Zofia growled impatiently, leveling the sword on him. "And this time, reach the other side, or don't bother coming back!"

"You can't make him do that again!" shouted Liza, her eyes brimming with tears as she ran to stand protectively in front of Carter, with Ernie and Enrique not far behind. "He already tried! He said it's impossible!"

Pirate Lady ignored her. "I'm counting to ten! And then I start eliminating—"

"STOP!" I shouted. "*Enough!* The heart isn't on the other side of that bridge!"

Five pairs of surprised eyes turned to stare at me.

"What are you talking about?" said Zofia. "Where is it, then?"

"Right here!" I pointed down at the stony platform—pointed all around us. "We're standing on it! Look around you!"

Everyone did. And a few seconds later, Liza, spinning in dizzy circles, shouted, "Jorge is right! It's right here!"

Not wasting a moment, the six of us dropped to our hands and knees and began clearing the rest of the dirt off the smooth reddish tiles.

And there, right at the very center of the huge, heart-shaped mosaic, I saw it.

"It's a keyhole!" I shouted. "We need a key! ¡Una llave!"

"I—I've never heard of any key," Ernie admitted, shaking his head. "Just that you have to stab the heart of greed. That's all the witch's riddle says."

"We must stab the heart of greed..." Zofia began mumbling under her breath. "Stab it. Stab it, we must!"

I glared up at her. "Hey, you're not helping any, Circus Yoda. Stab it with what?"

Suddenly all ten of Ernie's fingers tightened painfully around my arm. "Oh my gosh, Jorge!"

From the sound of his voice, I thought he'd forgotten to watch the latest Star Trek episode or something. Trust me, I'd seen this reaction before.

I shook my head at him. "What?"

"The heart's not really a heart, right? So then maybe the key's not really a key!"

"I repeat: *What?*"

"I'm talking about la bruja's dagger! The dagger is the key! Don't you get it? 'Stab the heart of greed'! You stab it with the dagger!"

I smacked my forehead. Of course! That made perfect sense! I remembered Ernie telling us that all three artifacts were required to discover the treasure of El Dorado—the sombrero, the witch's riddle, and that ancient dagger. And the dagger was the only one we hadn't used yet!

"Give him the dagger, already!" Enrique shouted at Zofia, and she did, quickly slipping it out of its jeweled sheath.

I didn't waste a second—I just jammed it straight into the keyhole, which not so surprisingly was a perfect fit!

At first, nothing happened, and we all sort of blinked at each other in confusion. But then there was a loud clunking sound, and the snapping, splintery protests of ancient wood . . . and suddenly, with a screeching groan, the forest of pendulum blades slowed their deadly swinging and creaked to a stop. Just like that!

And even better, the missing part of the bridge was now rising into place!

Look, da missing part of the bridge!

CHAPTER 46

"W-what is that thing?" I asked, trying not to look into its snarling black maw.

"That, dear children, is an ancient Aztecan sacrificial altar," answered Zofia with evil relish. "Its operation is quite simple, yet most effective. The offering is thrown into the mouth of the altar. If the offering is accepted, the mouth will close. If not, well, then you have to keep feeding it."

That's what I was afraid of, I thought.

She grinned evilly around at us now. "So which one of you would like to try to appease the altar first? I personally vote for the chupacabra. It's a very rare and splendid creature. It seems like a worthy sacrifice."

Ugh! I threw up my hands, beyond annoyed with

this treasure-hunting jerk. She made Bowser from Super Mario seem kindhearted! "You've got to be kidding!" I yelled.

"You can't do this!" Liza screamed at her.

"On the contrary, you can't stop me." Zofia wagged the glinting pirate saber in our faces like she was itching to use it on us. "It's either one of you or *all* of you."

"ENOUGH!" Enrique's voice boomed through the sacrificial chamber like an explosion, and immediately every eye in the place locked on him. "It will be me," he said quietly now. "I will be offered as the sacrifice. I was here when all of this started, and I will be here when it finally ends."

For several seconds all I could do was blink up at the sombrero in stunned silence. Had that self-absorbed, self-important, self-centered, self-serving, all-about-*me-me-me* sombrero really just offered to give himself up for us? Honestly, that might've been the most shocking thing that had happened down here yet.

"Enrique, you don't have to do that," Liza told him.

CHUPACARTER AND THE SCREAMING SOMBRERO

"Yeah, if she wants the treasure so bad, she can throw *herself* in!" Ernie agreed, glaring over his shoulder at Pirate Blackheart.

"Yeah, don't do it, dude." I paused for a second to swallow the sudden lump in my throat so my voice wouldn't crack. "She can't make us."

I almost couldn't believe the words that had just come out of my mouth. A few days ago, I would've happily thrown him into that altar myself! And I probably would've enjoyed it, too. But now... I don't know. I guess old leather-mouth had sort of grown on me.

You're right, Jorge— she can't make me. I choose to.

Enrique's voice was low now, choked with tears (or whatever bodily fluids got stuck in a hat's throat when it got all emotional). "Spending these past few days with the four of you, I have learned an awful lot about kindness and compassion. Watching how you all care about each other and how hard you try to make each other's lives better, I learned the true meaning of friendship, of family, and why it's so important to care about others and not just about yourself. I learned what true selflessness looks like. And during that same time, I realized something else, too. I realized that *all* of you have hearts of gold. All of you are worthy of the treasure. And that all of you would have done la bruja's will and given the treasure back to the people to whom it belongs."

"Well, maybe not *all* of it," I said, trying to make a funny, not really caring that a pair of tears were currently racing down my cheeks.

The sombrero smiled at me. "It was a pleasure riding on your giant cabeza, Jorge."

I put a hand gently on his brim—we all did. "We're going to miss you, amigo," said Liza, her voice shaking as tears welled in her sad, brown eyes.

"I'll never wear another sombrero," Carter whispered, sniffling.

"Me neither," agreed Ernie, wiping fresh tears from his face.

But, of course, like most beautiful moments, some selfish jerk had to come along and spoil it.

"Oh, for heaven's sake!" snapped Zofia, tearing Enrique off Ernie's head. "It's just a silly old hat! And an ugly one, no less!"

And with that, she reared back and flung Enrique into the dark, snarling mouth of the jaguar altar.

CHAPTER 47

For what felt like a long time the four of us just stood there, not saying anything. No joke, I felt like some witch had used a magic spell to turn my heart into a sheet of notebook paper and then ripped it right down the middle—ripped it in two. That's how awful I felt about what had happened to Enrique.

"Did it work?" Jan asked after a few tense moments.

The monster someone had mistakenly named Zofia gave a confused shrug. "I—I don't think so. Nothing's happened."

"Yeah, nothing except that you threw our friend into a bottomless pit!" I screamed, balling my hands into angry fists. "You selfish, greedy jerks! I hope nothing *does* happen! Actually, I hope this jaguar head magically comes to life and eats both of you, so you can see how it feels, you big bullies!"

Suddenly, the mountain began to quake. Cracks appeared in the stone walls, and rock dust crumbled down from the ceiling like sandy rain.

"I take it back! I take it back!" I shouted at the jaguar head in a panic. "Please don't come to life and eat anyone! I don't think I can handle that right now!"

Fortunately, it didn't come to life. But something even more mind-blowing happened!

Out of the open pit of the altar's mouth came ... a boy!

The moment he'd climbed out of the altar, all the quaking stopped and there was a soft grating sound as the jaguar's enormous stone-toothed maw ground slowly shut.

"The altar's vomiting up people!" shrieked Ernie. "It must've rejected the sacrifice!"

"¡Gente, soy yo!" shouted the boy. "It's me!"

I was about to say, "Me, who?" but that unmistakable voice gave him away.

"*ENRIQUE!*" we all shouted, leaping forward to throw our arms around him.

He was laughing so hard you'd think he just climbed out of the Laugh Factory. "You should've seen your faces when I came out! I can't believe you were so scared of little old me!"

"Yeah, just wait until *you* see someone come crawling out of a jaguar altar, and we'll see how your face looks," said Liza with a smirk.

"I knew it was you," said Carter. The big guy was all fangy smiles. "You still smell like goat leather."

That one made me lol.

A few feet away, Jan was looking at us like we'd all

just hatched from a dinosaur egg. "Talking chupacabras... sombreros transforming into people. You five are more fit for the circus than we ever were!"

"What's in your hand, boy?" Zofia asked Enrique. She pointed with her sword.

"What does it look like?" he replied with his usual snark. "A key."

"Where did you find it?"

"At the bottom of the altar. The one *you* threw me into. But I guess I should be thanking you, no? It broke the witch's curse! That brilliant hag had planned this from the very beginning. The moment I finally learned true selflessness, the spell she put on me was broken, just like she'd promised!"

"That's all very sweet," said Zofia, sounding like she really couldn't have cared less. "However, I'm still more interested in the *shiny* kind of treasure. What does that key open?"

"The door to the treasure room," said the former sombrero. "What else?"

CHAPTER 48

"La bruja told me I might one day run into someone like you, and she showed me the key before hiding it," Enrique explained as he closely inspected the wall of smooth bricks beside the jaguar head. "She told me that if a completely unworthy treasure hunter happened to make it this far, and if my curse had been lifted, I might as well lead you to the treasure."

Hidden in the wall behind a veil of antique spiderwebs was another enormous keyhole. The second Enrique slipped the key into it and, using both hands, cranked it like a submarine door, it was on like Donkey Kong. With the hiss of a thousand snakes and the whir of a thousand gears, the ancient stone doors that had for so long safeguarded the legendary treasure of El Dorado began to slowly rumble open on gigantic rust-caked hinges.

I'll give you exactly one guess at what we saw beyond those doors. But no offense, you'd probably guess wrong...

Sure, the room itself was pretty magnificent—a gigantic sprawling chamber about the size of Dodger Stadium, with a ceiling so high and so blanketed in absolute darkness that I almost imagined I could see tiny yellow stars twinkling way up there. I mean, it was everything you would expect a witch's private treasure vault to look like. Even the floors were paved with hundreds and hundreds of expensive-looking black-and-white marble tiles.

Except...

There was *no* treasure in it.

Like, *none*.

"Someone must've already found it," murmured Ernie, his voice thick with disbelief as he stared dazedly around at the empty chamber.

I blinked a bunch of times, but it didn't change what I was seeing—or rather, what I *wasn't* seeing. "I can't believe the treasure is gone."

"It's *not*. It can't be!" hissed Zofia, though it very obviously was.

"Kind of hard to argue with your own eyeballs, don't you think?" I said.

"Look! An exit!" Ernie pointed toward the far side of the treasure room, where a huge circular stone was rolling back to reveal something I thought I'd never see again: a glittering night sky! I could practically taste the fresh desert air gusting in.

"That's it!" I heard Liza whisper like the answer to some tricky exam question had just flown smack into her brain like a drunken honeybee. "*'Stab the heart of greed and seize the true treasure that lies before you!'* The exit is what needs to be seized! Life is the true treasure!"

Zofia, who apparently hadn't come to the same realization as Liza, raised the glinting edge of the pirate's sword threateningly to Enrique's neck.

"What went wrong? *WHERE'S MY TREASURE?*" she roared.

"There *is* no treasure!" Enrique explained. "La bruja probably destroyed it centuries ago! Don't you get it? It's just another one of the witch's tricks! She wants to teach greedy, treasure-obsessed people like you a lesson!"

All of a sudden, as if in response to his words, the entire cavern—no, the entire Tres Hermanas mountain range—began to shake like a giant tower of Jell-O!

Remember that exit I told you about? The one that had been rolling slowly open for us? Yeah, well, the big rock suddenly reversed course and was now grinding slowly *closed*. In other words: time to go!

I didn't need to convince anyone. Liza, Ernie, Carter, and Enrique immediately followed my lead, and the five of us took off across the treasure room like we had rockets strapped to our nalgas.

We had nearly reached the exit in the mountainside when a loud, piercing *ping!* had me slowing down, whipping my head around to look.

Ping, ping, ping-ping-ping!

Stuff was falling from the ceiling. Only it wasn't rocks or pieces of stalactites.

It was *TREASURE*!

Gold coins and silvers bars, rubies and emeralds and diamonds, dark blue sapphires the size of my fists, diamond-encrusted bracelets, glittering opal necklaces, pearls the size of baseballs, stunning gold

CHUPACARTER AND THE SCREAMING SOMBRERO

rings most likely forged in the fires of Mordor—everything!

All of it pouring steadily down from the dark ceiling of the treasure room like someone had taken the world's largest baseball bat to the world's most treasure-stuffed piñata.

"¡Vamos, Jorge!" Carter hissed, tugging frantically on my arm. "Da roof is crumbling!"

We took off running again and this time we didn't stop until we were only a couple steps from the exit.

"Hey! What are you two pea-brained pirates doing?" I shouted back at Zofia and Jan, who were scrambling around on their hands and knees, stuffing heaping handfuls of coins and jewels down the front of their shirts.

"No, don't go!" she shouted back, desperately waving us over. "Help us! I'll give you a cut of the treasure! We need more hands!"

Carter hopped back as a giant golden brick came slamming down between us, leaving a dent the size of Bigfoot's sneaker in the tiles.

Treasure was piling up faster than Tetris blocks, and I had a bad feeling the words GAME OVER were about to flash across the screen.

"Give it up already!" I screamed at the treasure-obsessed pirate wannabes. "This entire *mountain* is coming down!"

But were they listening to me? Not even a little. "Please, help us!" Zofia practically begged. "We need more hands! *PLEASE!*"

"Do you still not get it?! Your *life* is the true treasure! That's why all the challenges were so dangerous! The witch was trying to show the value of life and the dangers of greed! Open your eyes! The true treasure is right *there*!" I was pointing wildly at the exit, which, by the way, was about 80 percent closed now. "It's the way out of this place! Don't you understand? The treasure is a trap! It's the final challenge!"

I might as well have been talking to a wall. "Find a bag of some kind!" the circus lady shouted, giggling with glee. "Go to our car and empty our suitcases! Hurry now and fetch them so we can load up all this treasure!"

She was so completely oblivious to the gigantic masses of stalactites crashing down around her that she hardly even flinched when one nearly squashed her like a bug.

Man, some people never learn...

"Jorge, ¡vámonos!" yelled Carter, tugging on my arm. "It's almost closed!"

But just as I turned to run, another vicious earthquake rocked the mountain and my foot caught on the edge of some heavy crystal vase. I went down hard on my butt.

BROOOOMM

We made it. Just past the exit, we all went down in a tangle of arms and legs as the world rattled and quaked around us. And just as I tasted my first lungful of fresh New Mexican air, there was another earthshaking, world-breaking, reverberating *BOOM!* as what sounded like ten trillion tons of ancient priceless trinkets crashed down inside la bruja's mountain.

A few seconds later, from within the montaña came a very faint voice. "Hello? Can anyone hear us? We're kind of... *stuck*."

And, of course, we all burst out laughing.

"Guess they found a bit more treasure than they bargained for, huh?" I said.

"You can say that again!" Ernie snorted.

CHAPTER 49

"Well, it looks like we did it again, peeps!" said Liza, slinging an arm around our necks. "This time, though, with the help of a screaming sombrero."

Enrique gave a playful bow. "I humbly tip my hat to the four of you!" he said, and I couldn't help but laugh at that. I mean, the guy had *literally* been a hat up until twenty minutes ago.

"Nice one!" I stuck out my fist and Enrique gave me some skin while Carter gave us both some fur. "I've never met a cooler sombrero," I told him.

"I appreciate that, amigo. And I'll probably never meet a bigger head." He quickly held up his hands, grinning at me. "Just kidding! But I had to say it for old times' sake . . ."

From way off across the glimmering desertscape, on the other side of the Tres Hermanas mountains, I heard the unmistakable wailing of police sirens.

Liza glanced that way, her glasses glinting in the moonlight. "I guess my 911 text got through, after all."

"And I guess that's my cue to make a like tumbleweed and roll." Enrique looked around at us with a sort of bittersweet smile. "I don't want to be here when the police start asking questions. They probably won't believe me when I tell them what I've been up to for the last thousand years."

"Where are you going to go?" Liza asked him.

"Hachita. That's where I was born, and I've been wanting to visit for a long, *long* time."

Ernie frowned. "But isn't Hachita almost fifty miles away?"

"I wish it was five hundred! I'm more than a little eager to stretch these old legs!"

I couldn't blame him. I was actually surprised he still knew how to use them after all the centuries of hopping around on his brim.

"What are you going to do in Hachita?" Carter wanted to know.

Enrique shrugged like he was still weighing his options. "Probably take a job at the local school. I think I've lived through enough history to be able to teach it pretty well." His dark eyes sparkled in the night. "The funny part is, the first part of my life was cursed because of my selfishness. Now I want to spend the rest of my life giving to others."

"We'll come visit you," Ernie promised.

"I hope you do. It would be nice to see my friends again."

We all hugged it out one last time beneath the glow of a full and beautiful moon. It was cool.

"Hasta luego, amigo," I whispered, wiping someone else's tears off my cheeks. They couldn't have been mine. We Lopezes don't cry.

Enrique playfully punched me on the arm. "Nos vemos . . ." Then silently, like a shadow, he turned and started off into the cool night.

"See you!" Carter called after him, and I saw the outline of Enrique's hand lift in a small wave just as the beautiful Chihuahuan Desert wrapped her long shadowy arms around our new friend.

Out on State Road 11, the sound of sirens was growing steadily louder, and now I could see a line of flashing red and blue lights along the horizon.

For several moments the four of us just stood there, staring silently out at the approaching police cars, feeling the bright New Mexican moon smiling down on us—on everything.

Then, out of the blue, Ernie shrieked, "Oh, man, I just realized something! Even when the police dig the treasure hunters out, they'll never admit to anything! And the Aztecan dagger is way deep in there, stuck in the mosaic heart! So how in the world are we supposed to prove my dad's innocence?"

Aw, snap! Ernie was right! The dagger was basically the only hard evidence we had linking the treasure hunters to the museum robbery. And it wasn't like we could bring in our buddy Enrique as an eyewitness, because who would believe him?

We were basically back to square one!

"Relax," said Liza, slipping her phone out of her pocket. "I'm one step ahead of you guys. I recorded about half our adventure in here and Zofia's entire confession."

Total. Tidal wave. Of. Relief. That's the only way to describe what I felt right then. And even that was a fairly large understatement!

"That's why you're the eyes and ears of our operation, Liza!" I shouted, flinging an arm around her skinny shoulders. "That's why you're *you!*"

"Wait." Carter looked confused. "I thought I was da eyes and ears of da operation?"

"Nah, you're really more like the fangs." I said, which, naturally, Carter loved to hear.

"*WACHA!*" he cheered. "Dat's even *cooler!*"

Suddenly, a terrible bloodcurdling shriek ripped across the desertscape. "AAAAAAAAHHHHHH-HHHHHH!"

The four of us whipped around with our hearts in our throats to see Enrique standing there in the dark, maybe fifteen yards away. "What's wrong?!" I gasped.

"Oh, nothing," he said, grinning naughtily. "I just wanted to make sure I still had it."

EPILOGUE

PRICELESS TREASURE SOLD AT AUCTION

Mystery millionaires sell treasure at auction and donate all proceeds to help rebuild homes, libraries, and public parks in New Mexico's most economically distressed neighborhoods.

REAL THIEVES ARRESTED

Dad not guilty! How Boca Falls youths untangled a daring heist and proved a father's innocence!

CHUPACARTER AND THE SCREAMING SOMBRERO

CAN'T WAIT FOR ANOTHER ADVENTURE WITH CARTER AND THE GANG?

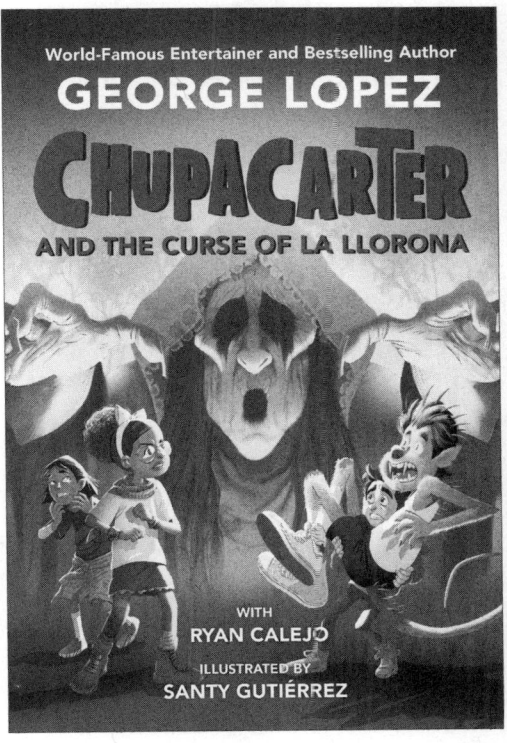

TURN THE PAGE FOR A SNEAK PEEK!

CHAPTER 1

Okay, okay, I'm lying.

That's not how it happened.

We weren't supersleuths and we didn't have an office with a view of Albuquerque and a cool bronze plaque.

But you'd be surprised how much trouble a kid from L.A. can get into when his mom sends him to the middle of Nowheresville, New Mexico, to live on his grandparents' farm. He could meet a chupacabra one night while sitting on his roof, moon watching.

They could become best friends. The chupacabra's name could be Carter.

Trust me, it *could* happen . . .

I know because it happened to me.

My name is Jorge Lopez, and I have a confession to make: my best friend is a seven-foot-tall bloodsucking monster, and ever since my mom sent me away to live a quiet, "normal" life, my life has been anything *but*. Just ask the talking sombrero we teamed up with to find the treasure of El Dorado last month. Or, if you think you're brave enough, have a lollipop and chat with the local haunted piñata. They'll tell you. If exercise is more your thing, go for a run with the killer vampire dogs called the dips... you're guaranteed to get a great workout with them!

Anyway, back to the sleuthing thing.

Like I said, my three best buds and I weren't professional detectives or anything like that. But word about some of the mysteries we'd solved had obviously gotten around, because we finally got our first "official" case.

It happened exactly one week after the last day of school. Liza, Ernie, Carter, and I were hanging out in the woods about a mile from my grandparents' farm on a warm, sunny afternoon, climbing trees and just generally goofing around. After everything we'd been through over the last few months, we were all hoping for a nice, peaceful summer.

Turns out, we were about to get anything *but*...

Somewhere behind me, I heard Ernie shriek,

"Aaaahhh! A chupacabra!" And Liza and I gave each other looks like, *Uh, you think he just noticed that about Carter now?*

But when we turned and spotted the huge, fur-covered, fang-faced monster—who, by the way, most definitely *wasn't* Carter!—the two of us started sounding an awful lot like our pal Ernie.

The monster waved and said hola, showing us a smiley mouthful of gleaming white fangs, which didn't help us feel any less scared. He politely introduced himself. I think he said his name was Pepe, but it was kind of hard to hear him over our shrieks and screams of panic.

"*Carter! Where's Carter?*" I shouted, looking frantically around for backup.

"¡Ah, sí!" the strange chupacabra grinned. "¿Dónde está Carter?"

Just then, the big guy dropped down from a mass of thick branches overhead, landing as gracefully as a cat right beside me. "Right here!" he said.

But suddenly he froze, his eyes narrowing suspiciously on the other chupacabra. "And I'm right *there*, too . . . ?" I could see the supernova of panic exploding in the brown depths of Carter's enormous eyes. "JORGE, HOW IS DIS POSSIBLE?" he cried.

"Carter, that's *not* you!" Liza tried to explain. "That's another chupacabra!"

At Liza's inarguable logic, the big guy seemed to relax. A fangy grin that would send any goat (and probably most people) running for its life spread across his furry face. "Dat make sense! Hola, Not-Me!"

Pepe the chupacabra waved a skinny, clawed hand in return. "¡Hola, Carter! ¡Es un honor! I've very much been looking forward to meeting you and your amigos!"

"You ... you've heard of us?" Ernie asked, sounding more than a little surprised as he peeked cautiously out from over my shoulder.

"¿Cómo no?" said Pepe with a sheepish giggle. "What chupacabra hasn't heard of Carter and his three amigos? You are all very famoso!"

"Famous for . . . *what*, exactly?" Liza wanted to know.

"For what?" Pepe looked at her like she'd just grown a third eyeball. "How about solving el misterio de la haunted piñata? Or finding the lost treasure of El Dorado!" Pepe was beaming at us now, happy as a mosquito at a blood bank. "I have to say, when I heard how the four of you gave all that treasure back to the people, I almost cried."

Whoa. So he really had heard of us. "Who told you about all that stuff?" I said, honestly curious.

Pepe laughed. "Gossip is not only a two-footer thing." I'm assuming "two-footer" was chupacabra slang for humans. "Forest animals talk, too."

"You're saying a little birdie told you?"

"Actually, it was a blue jay," said Pepe. He sounded like he might be telling the truth, too, so I decided not to poke any more fun. "Pajaritos get a nice bird's-eye view of the world and pass along mucha información."

Huh. That kind of made sense when you put it like that. (Note to self: make sure there aren't any birds flying by when you hide Grandma's cooking pot so she can't make her infamous pork stew.)

"Do you live around here?" Liza asked.

Pepe shook his shaggy head. "No. Mi familia y yo live very near the Sierra Pelona mountains."

"Hey, isn't that in Cali?" I said. "Right by Los Angeles?"

Pepe looked impressed. "You know those mountains?"

"Well, not *personally* or anything. But I'm from L.A."

"What are you doing way out here?" Liza asked the grinning chupacabra.

Suddenly that bright, fangy smile froze, dimmed, and fell into a deep, fangless frown. "My clan is in trouble," he revealed in a low voice. He sounded anxious now. Scared. And he looked it, too. "We are about to lose our ancestral home!"

CHAPTER 2

"Why? What happened?" Ernie asked Pepe.

The chupacabra shook his head sadly. "Nada. *Yet.* But I have seen the two-footers with the red vests. They came in great metal beasts with four round legs that spin and spin and spin. They studied our lands closely, all the way around, measuring them with their strange tools."

"You mean, like, surveyors?" said Liza.

"¡Sí! That is the word I heard Grandfather use! They were surveyors!" Now a sort of gloomy hopelessness filled the large, almond eyes. "They are going to destroy our tierra. Our woods. They are going to kill all the plants and animals and build enormous dead structures like the ones on that long road to the north." He was talking about the strip mall on Yucca Street. "The two-footers are coming, because Señor

Gomez can no longer protect us. That is what Abuelo said."

"Who's Señor Gomez?" Carter and I wanted to know.

"Maybe you should start from the beginning," Liza suggested.

Pepe didn't say a word for a good half a minute. He stared down at his giant clawed toes, as if deciding how much he could say without getting into trouble. When he spoke again, his voice was low and secretive. "My grandfather would not like me telling you all of this," he explained slowly. "I had to sneak away even to come here. He doesn't want me to get involved. He believes everything will turn out all right, but I know it won't. My grandfather is the elder of our clan and I do not like to disobey his wishes. The two-footer I told you about, Señor Gomez—he is my grandfather's friend. My grandfather has known him for many moons. He is also called Archie."

Ernie blinked in surprise. "Hold your seahorses. Are you talking about *Archie Gomez*, the famous movie producer?"

Pepe nodded like he thought so but wasn't sure. "I believe so. Señor Gomez makes pictures that *move*.

You can watch them on the talking boxes. I have seen some. They are very funny."

"Oh yeah, they're great!" said Ernie. "He makes some awesome horror movies, too! Like *Dorsal's Revenge!*" His excited eyes flicked to me. "You know, the one with the bottlenose dolphin that gets taken over by an alien parasite and starts eating spring breakers?"

I shook my head. "Nah, I don't watch scary movies. I get enough nightmares just living with my grandma."

"I don't understand," said Liza. "How is that movie producer involved?"

"It is his land we live on," Pepe explained. "He bought it to protect our home long ago."

"So, what happened? He's selling it now?"

"No, they are going to *take* it from him!" Pepe said ominously.

I frowned. "How come?"

"Because Señor Gomez's company is about to *die*."

"To die?" Carter didn't seem to like the sound of that.

"You mean, go bankrupt?" Liza asked Pepe, and the chupacabra nodded in a solemn, hopeless way.

"Sí. That is what Grandfather said."

Liza turned and those sharp brown eyes found mine. "The production company must be in debt.

Probably about to go belly-up, and the debtors must've hired surveyors to value his other holdings, which is where Pepe's home comes in. They're going to take it to help pay off his debt, most likely."

It made perfect sense. That had to be what was going on, but... "Uh, how do you think we can help you?" I asked Pepe.

From the pocket of his vest, the chupacabra brought out a crumpled sheet of paper and handed it to me. There were a bunch of words on it. Well, more specifically, jobs. The sorts of jobs you'd find on a movie set. And they were all spelled how they sounded, not how they were actually spelled, which made them kind of hard to read.

Those are the people who are about to be kidnapped!

READ ON IN...

AVAILABLE NOW!